I0686837

ADVANCES
OF THE
Ancients

R . N . C H E V A L I E R

Advances of the Ancients. Copyright © 2018 R.N. Chevalier. Produced and printed by Stillwater River Publications. All rights reserved. Written and produced in the United States of America. This book may not be reproduced or sold in any form without the expressed, written permission of the author and publisher.

Visit our website at www.StillwaterPress.com for more information.

First Stillwater River Publications Edition

ISBN-13: 978-1-946300-72-0
ISBN-10: 1-946300-72-1

1 2 3 4 5 6 7 8 9 10

Written by R.N. Chevalier

Published by Stillwater River Publications, Pawtucket, RI, USA.

The views and opinions expressed in this book are solely those of the author and do not necessarily reflect the views and opinions of the publisher.

In Memoriam
Tinamarie "Chevalier" Grow-Widener
29 July 1965–4 September 2015

Rest in peace, little sister.

To Donna Chevalier, the love of my life and my wife, and Jasmine Chevalier, my daughter.

Very Special Thanks
To Donna Chevalier for being the inspiration for Dutona Fental,
Tanya Guernon for being my Dinema Atany,
Daniel Guernon for inspiring Lieutenant Daniel.

Special Thanks
To my best friend, Dave Garneau, who, seventeen years
ago, helped me develop the board game, The Final Frontier.
Though the game was never produced, it became the
foundation of this novel.

Chapter 1

Jehovah sits in his command chair, waiting for an answer. The alien captain on the viewscreen shows a look of nervousness.

"Captain . . ." Jehovah's counterpart pleads. "Try to see it from my perspective."

"What perspective, B'Tong? You're a smuggler and a thief . . . and now you're a murderer."

"Captain, I assure you . . . it was self-defense."

"Not so, B'Tong," says first officer Commander Dinema Atany, the Utorian science officer who replaced Commander Lucifer, who remained on Terra to hunt the Niphillium six weeks ago. "The visual log you didn't know about clearly shows you firing your disruptor while the deceased was five meters away from you."

"Captain, the *deceased* was a scumbag arms dealer, not worthy of your trouble," B'Tong says, ignoring the female first officer yet answering her challenge.

"And you're the fucking dickhead that killed him," she responds defiantly.

Annoyance becomes anger on the face of B'Tong. Jehovah grins slightly, making sure his first officer doesn't see him.

"You disrespect me, and I'm going to call you out," she states blankly.

"Captain, we can surely come to some arrangement." A sly grin spreads across his face.

"Yes, we can. How about this?" Jehovah asks cautiously. "You beam over here and surrender yourself and I won't give in to my desire to blow your ship, your crew, and yourself straight to the bowels of hell." His tone becoming more pleasant as he speaks.

B'Tong gets visibly nervous, and his attention focuses on something out of visual range. He nods nervously as he looks back at Jehovah.

"Given those options, it appears my crew has decided to send me to you. So, therefore, I surrender. Prepare to beam me over. I surrender."

Jehovah keeps his eyes on B'Tong and says, "Tactical, keep all weapons locked on that ship until B'Tong is in the brig."

"Weapons locked and charged, Captain."

"Two minutes, B'Tong, two minutes."

"I'll be ready, Captain." The viewscreen changes, now showing the alien ship in the center of the screen, surrounded by stars.

"You have the bridge, number one," Jehovah says as he leaves the bridge, via the turbolift, heading for the transporter room.

The science officer assumes the center seat, adrenaline coursing through her veins in anticipation of the next few minutes.

Three minutes later, the ship rocks violently and the muffled sound of an explosion is echoing through the vents. The red-alert klaxon sounds.

"What the fuck?" Atany shouts with surprise. "Damage control, what happened?" She looks at the viewscreen to see B'Tong's ship starting to turn away.

"Disable their engines and weapons then lock them in a tractor beam," Atany says with a controlled anger in her voice. The weapons fire, and the ship on the screen rocks as its phaser emitter explodes. Another round of phaser fire takes out the engines, and the ship lists and starts to drift. A sparkling reddish beam emanates from a node on the *Heaven* and hits the damaged ship, holding it in place.

"Report coming in, Commander. Explosion on deck three, just outside of the transporter room," Lieutenant Roeton, the communications officer who replaced Lieutenant Kohath, who stayed with Lucifer on Terra, says, his voice sinking. Worry flows across the first officer's face. She walks briskly to the turbolift.

"I'll be back," Dinema says as she steps into the turbolift.

Atany exits the turbolift on deck three and heads down the hall. She turns right, toward the airlock, and sees the damage caused by the explosion that rocked the ship. The damage to the hall is moderate, but what lay on the floor is the most shocking.

Against the right wall is a bloody uniform that Atany recognizes as B'Tong's, and against the left wall is a bloody alliance uniform. There are large pools of blood surrounding various limbs and body parts.

Dr. Anak is examining the remains within the alliance uniform. From the rank insignia, she knows that it is Captain Jehovah. She cries visibly for several seconds. She pulls back the tears and lets the sadness turn to anger.

"Doctor, please inform me when the investigation is over," she says, straining to get the words out. Atany heads back to the turbolift for the bridge.

The doors of the turbolift open, and Atany walks out slowly, her head hanging down. She makes her way to the center seat. She starts to sit and feels the eyes of the room burning into her. She sits and straightens up.

"Put me on ship-wide intercom," she says.

"Channel open," comes from behind.

"Attention, all hands. This is Commander Dinema Atany. Several minutes ago, you all felt an explosion rock the ship. An investigation is ongoing, but I must inform all hands that Captain Jehovah was killed in that explosion. So, as of now, stardate two, nine, nine, three, five point nine, seven, I am assuming command of this vessel. Note it in the log."

There is a brief pause as everyone absorbs the news of the captain's untimely death. To all on the bridge, everything starts moving in slow motion. Seconds pass, feeling like hours. Time catches up to itself and everyone else.

"Hail that ship," Atany says, her words thick with anger.

"They have been trying to hail us for five minutes," replies Lieutenant Roeton. "Channel open, Captain."

The alien first officer is now on the screen.

"What?" Dinema's voice is slow and strong. She stands tall and steady.

The alien first officer is visibly nervous and hesitates slightly.

"Captain, B'Tong was a fool." Fear is thick in his voice. "His death was inevitable."

"Make your point."

"We would like to bargain for our release."

"What could you possibly have that would be of interest to me?"

"Have you ever heard of the Forzak Empire?" A sly grin sweeps across his face, and his eyes widen.

"Everyone's heard of the Forzak Empire. What does that have to do with any of this?"

"Well . . . several days ago, while waiting for an acquaintance on a small, uncharted asteroid—and quite by accident, I assure you— we came into possession of a very old artifact that we believe makes reference to them. We allow you to study the artifact, and when you confirm its authenticity, you could . . . let us go?"

She thinks for a moment. "You will bring it here, and when we authenticate it, we will consider your offer. We will beam you over momentarily."

A look of relief comes across the alien's face as the viewscreen goes back to the ship and stars.

"Scan their data files," Atany says to tactical officer Sacar, who replaced Lieutenant Simeon, who stayed on Terra with Lucifer's team.

"I wanna know everywhere that ship has been for the last two weeks."

Aye, ma'am." He says as he starts the scan.

"Transporter room reports prisoner aboard," Roeton interrupts.

"Have security bring that fucker up here."

"Files scanned, ma'am. The data you requested is in secured data storage," Sacar reports.

"All right then. Lock all weapons on that ship, and standby."

"Weapons locked" is heard just as the turbolift doors open. The alien officer walks to the center of the bridge, in front of the new captain. He hands an unusual object to Atany.

She takes it from his hand and looks it over carefully. "So you are the new captain?" she asks. "The one I negotiate with?"

"Yes, ma'am, I am." He smiles, and Dinema sees him relaxing.

She turns to Sacar. "Give me a forcefield," she says as she makes a circular motion around the alien officer.

"Aye, ma'am," she replies. "Engaged." The shimmering red haze of the forcefield envelopes the alien from floor to ceiling.

"What's the meaning of this?" he demands angrily. "We have a deal!"

"Hear this, asshole!" Atany says firmly in a slightly raised voice. "I don't give a fuck about B'Tong, but the explosion killed my captain as well. For that, all I can say is . . . Fire!"

Weapons fire destroys the ship on the viewscreen.

"What the fuck?" the alien yells.

"Oh," she continues more calmly, "one more thing."

"Fuck you!" he screams defiantly.

"Okay, then," she says, suddenly and weirdly relaxed. "Transporter room, beam this miserable piece of shit into space."

"What!" A look of terror and surprise shows on his face as he fades away in the transporter beam's sparkling blue glow.

"Now maybe these fucking pirates will think twice before they mess with alliance ships. Get us to starbase nine," the first officer says as she sits in the center seat.

> *Captain's log. Stardate 29936.28. After Captain Jehovah's memorial service, I met with alliance command and was promoted to captain and given permanent command of the* Heaven *to pursue the truth about the "Forzak Artifact", as it has now become known. Procouncil Jacorrian has given me the widest possible berth and discretion to do whatever I see fit to do to secure the secret of the Forzak Empire.*

Atany sits in her ready room. The communications panel on her desk beeps twice, then, "Channel open, ma'am. Procouncil Jacorrian on the line, and line is secure." The panel chimes twice again.

"AtTionne. Do you have the information I asked for?"

"I sure do. The foremost specialist on the legend of the Forzak Empire is Professor Aristotle Hawking. He was last seen in the Brantax star system, but that data is ten days old."

"At least it's a starting point. Thanks for your help. I'll keep you in the loop. Out." She reaches to deactivate the panel.

"Not so fast," he interrupts, and she stops suddenly. "There's one more thing . . . and it's not good."

"It never is. Go on."

"Word has already gotten out, and our intelligence operatives have confirmed that the Chandraka and the Rillians have dispatched ships to intercept you," he says, somewhat apologetic.

"Great . . . lizards and bugs. What the fuck? What about the Horatha?"

"What about the Horatha?" he replies. "We can't get operatives close enough, but you'll have to count on seeing them eventually, considering what's at stake."

"Right on, AtTionne. Good health to you." She deactivates the panel.

The captain comes onto the bridge from her ready room and takes her seat. One by one, each crewman looks at her, awaiting her next orders. She takes several breaths.

"Helm, how long will it take us to get to the Brantax system at warp six?" she asks.

"Nine hours and forty-two minutes," Lieutenant Levi says after a few seconds.

"Good. Plot a course and get us there."

"Yes, ma'am," he says as he manipulates the controls in compliance.

"Roeton," she says. "Ship-wide intercom."

"Channel open," he answers.

"All hands, this is the captain." She starts speaking calmly and slowly. "We are now heading to the Brantax system to find the foremost specialist on the legend of the Forzak Empire. We also have the pleasure of future encounters with the Rillians and the Chandraka as they are on their way, and the Horatha can't be far behind. From now on, we will be on yellow alert. Stay sharp and focused on the mission and we'll be fine. Out." She slices her extended thumb across her throat, and Roeton, picking up on her signal, switches the intercom off.

"Polarize the hull plating and find a way to enhance long-range sensors. When the others come to play, I want as much warning as possible." She continues in the same calmness.

"Hull plating polarized," Lieutenant Sacar, at tactical, replies. "Long-range sensors enhanced by forty-six percent."

"Outstanding," she responds as a wide smile blossoms on her face, causing her smoothly chiseled features to round out and expose her dimples. She sits back, relaxed from confidence.

"Captain, we will be in the Brantax system in one hour," Lieutenant Merah, the night-duty helmsman, says aloud.

"Excellent," she replies. After a moment, she spins her chair to face the communications officer. "Reuben, contact security and have them send two officers to the observation lounge."

He silently complies.

"I'll be in the observation lounge," she says aloud as she gets up and goes through the doors on the right side of the bridge.

The captain enters the lounge, and just as she sits, a man and a woman enter the room from the doors at the opposite side of the room. As the two approach the captain, the man steps ahead of the woman, visibly nudging himself ahead of her.

"Lieutenant Abaddon reporting as ordered." The male officer's mannerisms and protocols are one hundred percent military standard, so much so that the captain has to hold back the chuckle she wanted to let out. After returning the young archangel's salute, she turns to the female lieutenant, half hidden by her male counterpart. As the captain turns to see the officer, she hears, "Lieutenant Fe—"

"Fental!" the captain says, surprise in her voice. "Dutona Fental!"

The lieutenant turns to the captain with a look of surprise.

"Holy crap! Dinema! I heard you were doing well, but captain? Wow!"

They notice Abaddon, and Fental snaps to attention and salutes. The captain returns her salute.

"We'll catch up later. Have a seat." She motions to the chairs at the table nearby. "And relax." The three sit.

"We'll be arriving in the Brantax system within the hour," Atany starts.

"Our first stop is Brantax Eleven. You both know its reputation?"

They nod in agreement.

"That is why the two of you are here. I will be going down to Brantax Eleven to find Professor Hawking. The two of you are coming down to watch my back. Any questions?"

Both remain silent.

"Good," the captain continues. "Then get ready, and I will call when it is time to beam down. Dismissed." The two get up to leave.

"Oh, Fental," the captain says with a smile. "Stay please."

The lieutenant, smiling back as she sits, answers, "All right."

Abaddon leaves.

"So, how long has it been?" the captain asks as she retrieves two cups of hot tea from the replicator.

"About five years," Fental replies as Atany puts the cup down on the table in front of her. "Thank you," she responds as the captain sits.

"I didn't know you were on the *Heaven* when I put in for this assignment," Fental says. "Never mind, Captain. Sorry about Jehovah. I was looking forward to serving under him. Sucks how you got the job, but congrats." There is sorrow in her voice.

"Yeah, makes me sick how I got it, but shit happened. The only question I couldn't answer was whether that fuckhead B'Tong targeted the captain personally or his crew killed him in hopes of escaping us. That is my lingering regret."

"Why couldn't you get an answer?" Fental asks.

"Everyone involved died."

"Died?"

"Died."

"Shit."

"Yep . . . but what about you?" Atany says with some pep in her voice and a smile, trying to lift the mood in the room. "When we met at the fairgrounds, you weren't sure about joining. You wouldn't even hold my weapon."

"Yeah, it still took a while before I signed up. What's funny is, I got a perfect score on my weapons qualifications."

"How did you manage that?" Atany asks with a slight giggle.

"The right instructor, I guess. A lieutenant named Daniel, for H'Too Bar'klaa. The most easygoing guy you ever met. I was so afraid of weapons because I didn't know anything about them, but Lieutenant Dan explained how they worked, showed me the proper procedures, and trained me from small arms all the way up to the MX-1903 assault phaser."

The captain smiles a particular smile.

"You know him?" Fental asks.

"Yeah," she answers, still smiling. "I know him." She takes a slight pause to collect her thoughts. "When did you come on board? I didn't see your name on the duty roster, and why security? I saw you in science or medical."

"Yesterday, at Gurnin station, during your resupply layover, I'm replacing someone who stayed behind on Terra. I was into science, as a matter of fact. I spent my senior academy year and the better part of last year as night-duty science officer on the Leco."

"You were on the Leco?" Atany asks with some amazement. "Were you on board during the attack?"

"Yes, yes, I was." Fental takes a breath and starts softly, "It happened at thirteen hundred hours. I was in the mess hall because I couldn't sleep. Had I been in my quarters, we wouldn't be having this conversation right now. Anyway, I made it to an escape pod, and two weeks later, eight of us were picked up. That's when I figured security would be safer." She starts to laugh.

"That's fucked up, but I'm really glad you were one of the eight."

"So am I." They raise their tea cups for a toast. "So am I."

The chirp of the communications panel interrupts their continued conversation. The captain activates the unit.

"What is it?" she asks.

"We have been cleared and are entering standard orbit around Brantax Eleven," the disembodied voice responds.

"Then it's show time. Have Lieutenant Abaddon meet us in the transporter room. Out." The two women get up and head to the transporter room.

The sparkling blue haze fades, and the three alliance officers are standing in the courtyard of the twelve-story, three-acre square building that houses the central government of Brantax Eleven. They enter the front doors of the glass facade that is the front of the building and stand in a huge lobby. They approach the central information desk at the far end of the room and address the concierge.

"My name is Captain Dinema Atany of the alliance starship *Heaven*. I need to find the whereabouts of Professor Aristotle Hawking."

"Give me a minute to check the transit logs," the middle-aged man behind the counter says as he taps away on his terminal's keyboard. After about a minute, he says, "Ahh, here we go. Professor Hawking left here six days ago and is currently at the Maroonna archeological dig site on Brantax Three."

"Can we have his exact coordinates, please?" Atany asks politely.

"Certainly," he says cheerfully as he keys in more commands. "The coordinates have been uploaded to your vessel, and confirmation has been received."

"Thank you very much. Good health to you," Atany says as the three start to walk away.

As the huge front doors open, the three are standing face-to-face with five Rillians with very bad attitudes.

"What the fuck?" Atany asks with surprise.

"What?" the lead Rillian says with the same surprise. "It's them! Grab them!"

"Break!" Atany shouts, and the three officers spin and head in different directions. They find cover and draw weapons. The Rillians enter the lobby and spread out, weapons already drawn.

Lieutenant Abaddon fires and hits one of the soldiers square in the chest. The insectoid lets out a scream of pain as it falls. Captain Atany fires, but her target moves behind a large potted plant, which promptly explodes when the high-intensity beam from her phaser hits it. The hidden soldier is thrown from his spot and manages to hide behind a pillar.

Lieutenant Fental takes aim from behind a pillar and takes out the soldier at the far right, partially hidden in an alcove by the elevators. She spins her body to the right and takes out the one the captain missed.

Atany takes out the fourth soldier as Fental scores a direct head shot on the leader of the group, its head exploding before it could make a sound, spraying gooey green gobs of brain matter, or guts, over the wall behind it.

There is a brief moment of silence before the three alliance officers come out into the open to assess the situation.

"How did you learn to shoot so good?" Atany asks with a little sarcasm in her voice as they approach the bodies on the lobby floor.

"The ginger ninja," Fental answers, and Atany laughs out loud.

"The what?" she asks, still laughing.

"Lieutenant Dan, the academy instructor. He gave me private lessons. He is very good."

"I know," the captain says. "But why 'ginger ninja'?"

"Well, apart from being the weapons instructor, he is the self-defense instructor. He also has reddish blond hair. Hence the name ginger ninja."

"That's funny," Atany says. "I'll have to remember that."

"All five are dead, Captain," Abaddon reports. He then turns to Fental and says, "Excellent shooting, excellent indeed."

The three walk outside. The captain flips the lid of her communicator and says, "Captain to *Heaven*, three to beam up." As she closes the lid of the device, they hear the hum of the annular confinement beam as their bodies start to dematerialize.

"Levi, set a course for Brantax Three. One-half impulse. Go to the coordinates sent by the concierge," Atany says as she comes out of the turbolift and approaches her seat.

"Aye, ma'am" is all he replies as he carries out her command.

She spins her chair to face the science station, preparing to ask a question. "Fuck," she says softly to herself when she realizes the day-duty science officer, her previous position, hasn't been replaced. She sits back and thinks a moment. She turns to the communications officer.

"Roeton, have Lieutenant Dutona Fental report to the bridge."

"Yes, Captain," he answers. It took about six minutes before the turbolift doors open and Fental steps onto the bridge and in front of the captain, visibly nervous.

"Lieutenant Fental reporting as ordered," she says, speaking as nervously as she looks.

"Relax, Fental," the captain says calmly. Fental relaxes, and the captain continues, "When we talked earlier, you told me you were science officer on the Leco, yes?"

All eyes on the bridge face the two women.

"Yes, Captain," she answers.

"That's a good thing."

"I don't understand."

"Well, due to some bureaucratic bullshit, it appears I am short one science officer. The job is yours."

"But, Captain."

"No worries, Fental. I know you can do it, and I need you."

She remains silent for a long second. "You got it, Captain." She smiles as she heads to her new station.

The captain smiles back. She sits in her seat to acclimate to her new position. Her acclimation time is short.

"Now, Lieutenant." The captain turns to her new science officer. "For the first order of business, I want all the known data on the Maroonna archeological site on Brantax Three and what Professor Hawking could be interested in."

She turns to Levi. "Helm, how long before we arrive on Brantax Three?"

"Twenty-two minutes," he replies.

"You have fifteen minutes, Fental."

"Fifteen minutes," Fental reiterates with amusing sarcasm. "No pressure. No problem. By your command." She buries her face in the monitor as everyone giggles lightly.

Thirteen and a half minutes later . . .

"Captain," Fental begins, "the Maroonna archeological site was discovered seven months ago. It is a city calculated to be one-twentieth excavated so far. It is calculated to be one thousand one hundred years old. There is not enough data to speculate what Professor Hawking would want here."

"Never mind," Atany says. "I know why he's here."

"Care to enlighten us?" Dutona asks.

"He's looking for information on the Forzak Empire. The site is dated to the time the empire existed. Let's hope he's found something by now." She looks at Levi. "How long?"

"Five minutes," he answers.

"Captain, we are being hailed by central command." Lieutenant Roeton breaks the silence. "We have clearance to enter orbit."

"Tell central command that we are going into geosynchronous orbit above the dig site."

Roeton complies. "Request received and approved," Roeton replies. "One more thing, Captain. Central command wants you to tell alliance command to expect a bill for the mess they had to clean up on Brantax Eleven," his voice exposing his confusion.

Atany and Fental look at each other and laugh.

"Helm, bring us into orbit."

The starship glides into a gentle path over the planet's atmosphere to the coordinates given by the concierge on Brantax Eleven.

"I'm beaming down," the captain says as she stands and turns toward the turbolift. "Fental, you're with me."

The two women enter the turbolift.

"Grab a couple of phasers and communicators from the locker," the captain tells Fental as they walk down the hall toward the transporter room. They enter the transporter room, and Fental gets the equipment from the locker. The captain turns to the transporter chief.

"Keep a lock on us at all times," she says. "At the first sign of trouble . . ."

"Understood, Captain," the operator replies.

The women step onto the platform and sparkle into nothingness.

The archeological dig site in the Maroonna region of Brantax Three is a barren place. The wind blowing off the eastern desert is just over one hundred degrees. A millennium ago, this same area was a lush region at the conjunction of four rivers with several hundred species of animals.

From their beam-down point, the two women can see a rectangular hole about two thousand acres square and just over twenty feet deep. Looking out over the vastness of the hole, they see three spires rising from the bottom of the hole and up forty feet above the ground the women are standing on.

In the vast hole are rooftops of many more smaller buildings connected by narrow roads. Some of the buildings have been cleared of the centuries of windblown sand that filled them. Others are being emptied by teams of workers.

"There are three hundred workers down there," a voice from behind says.

The two women spin around in a flash and are facing the owner of the voice with phasers pointing at his face.

"Hey! Hey!" the man says in a panic with his hands blocking his face in a defensive stance.

The women relax and holster their weapons.

"Sorry about that," Atany says apologetically.

"Is there something I can do for you lovely ladies, or are you just out sightseeing?"

"I'm Captain Dinema Atany of the starship *Heaven*. This is Lieutenant Dutona Fental. We are looking for Professor Aristotle Hawking. Any ideas?"

"Ahh, Professor Hawking. He is in the building on the far left," the man says as he points to the building in question. "You will find him in the subbasement."

"Thank you," Atany says politely as she takes out her communicator and flips the lid. "Transporter room. Lock onto the rooftop of the large building south of our location and beam us there." The two are instantaneously moved to the roof.

The captain looks around and heads to the hatch in the middle of the roof. Atany slowly lifts the hatch lid while Fental aims her phaser into the dusky light. Finding it clear, they climb down the ladder.

From the ladder there are four halls running all the way to the outer walls. On each side of each hall are evenly spaced arched entryways leading into a series of rooms, all cloaked in darkness. At the end of the north wall is a door. The two women move quickly to the door and cautiously open it.

On the other side of the door is a stairway spiraling down into the foreboding darkness.

"After you." Fental gestures for Atany to lead.

"Oh, no," Atany says, smiling. "Captain's prerogative. You first."

Fental takes the lead, and the two start down. They get down to the bottom of the stairway and find a door.

"I guess this is the subbasement," Fental says.

"Then let's get Hawking and get this show on the road," Atany replies.

The two open the door and find a hall running along the entire length of the building in both directions. Directly across from them is an archway leading into a chamber. From the light coming through the door, they can see that the chamber is about twenty meters deep. There is an archway on the far wall leading to another chamber. Its also hidden by darkness. There are evenly spaced archways spread along the inside wall of the hall in both directions.

"Which way, Captain?" Fental asks.

Atany puts her hand up slowly with a finger pointed up. After about ten seconds, she answers. "This way," she says, motioning to her left. The two start walking down the hall, and about two-thirds of the way down the hall, roughly sixty meters, they hear sounds coming from an inner chamber.

They enter the chamber and head toward the back wall. The voices get louder with each step they take. They pass through two other chambers then see a faint glow coming from an archway on the right wall.

"A few more chambers and we should find them," Atany says.

"Yeah," Fental agrees. "But I sure hope we can find our way out of here."

"One thing at a time," Atany says as they turn a corner into a brightly lit chamber. They stop quickly, surprised at what they see.

The three men standing by the west wall turn to face the noise coming from behind. They see the two women standing there.

"Sorry to interrupt, but I need to speak to Professor Aristotle Hawking."

"Ari," the man on the left says as he turns his head slightly. "You have company."

The two women turn their attention to the movement coming from the shadows of the next chamber over.

"What are you talking about, Shawn?" a man says as he enters the chamber. "What's this abou—" He pauses as he appears visibly startled.

"Oh! Hello there," he says to the two women. They both show a smile of agreement. At six feet three inches tall, husky but not fat, with dark hair and hazel eyes, both women find him appealing.

"Professor Hawking?" the captain asks.

"Yes," he says with a smile. "I am Professor Hawking. And you are?"

"I am Captain Dinema Atany. This is Lieutenant Dutona Fental. We are from the alliance starship *Heaven*, and we need your help."

"What can I do for the alliance?" His face is showing confusion.

Atany takes out a padd and calls up an image. She hands it to him. "Do you recognize any of these symbols?" she asks.

After several seconds of studying the symbols, Hawking's eyes grow wide, and a huge smile spreads across his face.

"This is remarkable!" he says, excitement flowing in his words. "Where did you get this, Captain?"

"We came across it inadvertently. I know it's part of a larger artifact, but we don't have the rest yet, though we might be able to find where that piece was located," she answers. "Now, Professor, do you recognize any of the symbols?"

"Shawn!" he shouts, ignoring her question. "Call up the images we took on Zareth last year. Quickly!"

Shawn brings a padd over to Hawking and holds it up for him to see.

"Not that one," Hawking snaps slightly. "Go over a few more."

Shawn slides his finger across the screen, and the image changes. Hawking nods no, so he changes to the next image. After a few more swipes, Hawking's eyes suddenly get wide.

"That's it!" he shouts. "That's the one." While moving his finger from one image to the next, he says, "Look at these . . . see how the glyphs line up here and here?"

"Yes," Shawn confirms. "I see it. And look here. See how this glyph is predominate above this one but is in the background over here? These can only be spatial coordinates."

"Yes! Exactly!" Hawking says then turns his attention to the women. "Where exactly did you get this?"

"We retrieved it from pirates. We didn't get a chance to find out where they got it."

"Fuck!" Hawking screams. "To be so close!"

"Why is the location so important?" Fental asks.

"The spatial coordinates must be calculated from Zareth and the location where this artifact was found. That's the way we believe the Forzak calculated positions, triangulating from two reference points."

"We have the flight plan of the pirate ship in our data banks," Fental volunteers to the group.

"You do? That's awesome," he says, excitedly. After a second, a look of confusion comes across his face. He turns to the captain. "In all the excitement and distraction, Captain, something has eluded me," he says.

"The reason for our visit?" she speculates.

"Yes, exactly. The reason for your visit." He hands her padd back to Fental.

"My mission is simple, Professor. I have been ordered to find the homeworld of the Forzak Empire," she says slyly, almost seductively.

Hawking's face starts to glow as his eyes grow large and a smile sweeps across his face. He takes a deep breath.

"Well, isn't that advantageous?" he says giddily.

"What do you mean, Professor?"

"Shawn," he says, again ignoring the captain's question. "You're in charge here. I will send the rest of the artifact's symbols to your padd. I'm going to take the padd from here and the one from Zareth."

Hawking looks back at Atany and Fental, who are now visibly annoyed by his inconsiderate attitude, and he sees it.

"I'm so sorry." The sincerity in his voice is authentic. "When I get excited, I forget my manners. I didn't mean to ignore your questions." He pauses for a second then continues, slower this time. "I'm looking for the Forzak. You're looking for the Forzak. I'm going with you two." Smiling as he explains.

The two women look at each other and smile. They look back at the professor.

"Welcome aboard," Atany says after a few seconds of thought.

Chapter 2

Captain's log, stardate 29950.44. Professor Aristotle Hawking, the foremost expert on the legend of the Forzak Empire, has come aboard to assist in our quest, and we have made some headway in our search. I think Professor Hawking will be invaluable on this mission. And, on a personal note . . . he's not bad to look at.

"Okay, Professor," Atany says after the doors to Hawking's quarters close. "I know it's only been two hours, but can you give me some idea of where to go?"

"You can head to Zareth while I try to decipher these glyphs," he answers as he looks up from the artifact.

"Any luck so far?" she asks as she steps closer to the professor.

"A little, but nothing that makes much sense right now. I will let you know when I've made any progress."

"Right on. I'll be on the bridge when you need me." She turns and walks toward the door.

"Captain."

She stops and turns her head to face him.

"I just have to tell you, you are a very beautiful woman."

"Thank you," she says as a slight flush spreads across her face and a smile starts forming on her lips.

"I'll contact you when I have something to report." He looks back down at the artifact.

"Call any time," she replies as she walks out into the hall, the smile widening across her face as the door closes behind her.

The turbolift doors open onto the bridge. Atany steps out and takes her seat. A yeoman comes up to her with a padd of daily reports, the mundane aspect of command. She reviews and approves them. She turns to the helmsman.

"Lieutenant Levi, set a course for Zareth, warp three."

"Yes, ma'am," he replies as he sets the control.

"What's our ETA?"

"Six hours, eighteen minutes."

"What would our ETA be at warp five?"

"Four hours, four minutes."

"That's better," she says. "Increase to warp five."

"Warp five, aye," Levi repeats as he executes the command.

"Very good," Atany answers. She sits back and allows herself to fall deep into thought. After about a minute, a sly smile spreads across her face.

The next three and a half hours finds everything running smoothly. The night-duty rotation has been on for an hour, yet the captain sits fast, patiently waiting for their arrival at Zareth, or word from Professor Hawking. All is quiet.

"Captain," Lieutenant Reuben, the communications officer, breaks the silence. "Professor Hawking would like to speak to you."

"Okay. Pipe it through done here," she orders, and the light on the armrest panel lights up. She presses the button beside the light. "Yes, Professor?"

"How long until we reach Zareth?" Hawking's disembodied voice asks.

"Thirty-three minutes," Levi answers.

"Did you get that, Professor?" Atany asks.

"Yes, Captain, I did," he answers, then asks, "Can you come to my quarters? I found something."

"I'll be right down, Professor." She stands and heads into the turbolift.

"Come in," Aristotle says after the door chime sounds.

Atany enters when the door opens and approaches the desk where the professor is working.

"Ah, Captain, good morning," he says excitedly.

"It's not morning, Professor," she replies with puzzlement in her voice.

"It is somewhere in these universes," he retorts.

"Touché" is all she can say.

"Captain, I need to know where you acquired this artifact."

"We don't know exactly."

"Please explain."

"I got it from a pirate just before I killed him. I don't know where he got it, but we have all the ship's navigational data in our computer."

"We need to find out exactly where this was found." He points to the artifact. "We need to find the rest of it. When we find the rest of that piece and with what we'll find on Zareth, I'll have a better idea of what to do next."

"How do you know we'll find something on Zareth?"

"The glyphs on that artifact make reference to the Forzak and what I believe is Zareth, but I don't know why. And if my theory of multiple reference points for plotting courses through space is correct and we can find the rest of the artifact, we'll have three locations that reference the Forzak to work with. With that we may find more clues and then . . ."

"The Forzak homeworld," she finishes and then continues, "Now, what are we supposed to do when we get to Zareth? What are we supposed to be looking for?"

"That's what I called you about," he starts. "What we found on Brantax Three and Zareth are glyphs on walls. The piece you have is part of something else, something that we haven't found on either planet. This piece emits a low-level old-style radio wave."

"What a minute," Atany interrupts. "How can it do that?"

"Exactly." His eyes wide with excitement. "I haven't figured that out yet. What I do know is that the signal strength is low enough that the sensors will have to be set at narrow beam. I know it will take a while, but it's the only way."

"It'll take at least a day, at least, to scan on narrow beam," she informs the professor. "But I'm guessing you already knew that."

"Yes, yes, I did, but think of the rewards, Captain."

"I have three other things to think about, Professor," she reminds him. "The Rillians, the Chandraka, and the Horatha."

The *Heaven* glides into a standard orbital pattern above Zareth to start the long assignment.

"Set for narrow beam scan from the northern pole to the southern pole in two-degree increments," the captain orders lieutenant Korah, the night-duty tactical officer.

"Narrow beam?" Korah questions. "Two degrees per pass? That'll take over a day."

"I know. It is the only way," she says soothingly.

"Captain," Hawking, standing by Fental's science station, interrupts. "Sorry to interrupt, but may I make a suggestion?"

"Go for it," Atany replies.

"We can assume they would put any artifact around where they would write about it, so start at the coordinates of my dig site and work in an outward spiral. That may cut down on time."

"That's fucking brilliant," Atany says then turns to Korah. "Start at the dig site."

"Oh," Hawking interrupts again. "The signal is fourteen point eight five decahertz. Thought you might want to know."

For two and a half hours, the scans reveal nothing. The captain and professor walk over to Fental's station and lean in close.

"We need to review the flight data from B'Tong's ship. We need to isolate the places he could have picked up that artifact."

Dutona keys in some commands, and the monitor in front of them comes to life with an image of the local region. A blue line going from left to right in a zigzag pattern shows the path of the pirate ship for the last two weeks before its fateful encounter with the *Heaven*.

"We know where the ship was, but how do we determine where the artifact was picked up?" Hawking asks.

Fental looks at the captain. "It's in what he said," she says after several seconds of thought.

"Two things," Atany starts. "It was several days before our encounter, and he said they found it on a small uncharted asteroid."

Fental and Hawking simultaneously put their fingers on the right side of the blue line and trace it backward. Several inches to the left, they see a small deviation.

"Here, what's this?" Hawking asks aloud.

"Let's find out," Dutona says as she keys in commands. In seconds, a white crosshair symbol appears on the screen and inches its way to the point the three are looking at. The symbol blinks twice, and the area within the crosshair explodes with magnification. The small deviation nearly fills the screen.

"This is the place," Dutona says. "Their sensor log shows a rogue asteroid at coordinates two, six, one by three, four, eight by one, one, seven. Shows they were there for nine hours."

"Then when we're done here, we'll go there," Atany announces.

"The coordinates are locked in the computer and ready for helm control," Fental adds.

"Very good, Lieutenant."

Two hours later finds the captain in her cabin, unsuccessfully trying to get some sleep. The communications console on her desk beeps, and she sluggishly makes her way to it. She hits the switch as she sits down.

"What is it?" she asks while she rubs her eyes.

"We've picked up a faint signal," Lieutenant Aaron, the night-duty science officer, answers. "We should have the coordinates by the time you get up here."

"I'll be up ASAP," she says, starting to perk up quickly.

The doors of the turbolift open. Atany steps onto the bridge, followed by Dutona, who takes her station. Lieutenant Aaron takes the seat to the left of Fental, assisting in the analyzing the data.

"Where are we on that signal?"

"Coordinates on the main viewscreen, Captain, but I can only zero in within one square kilometer," Aaron says as a bright-green dot starts flashing on the image of Zareth, the dot indicating the coordinates of the signal.

"Why? What's the surrounding terrain like?"

"Sensors show mountainous terrain littered with deep caves and deeper caverns," Fental answers.

"Where exactly is that signal coming from?" There is a long silence.

"Fental? Signal?"

"Just a second, Captain. I'm having issues zeroing in."

"Issues? What issues?"

"Ah, got it," Fental starts. "The signal is coming from two kilometers below the surface."

"In a cave?"

"Yes."

"Why haven't they found it yet?" Hawking adds. "All these caves have been searched and mapped."

"I know why," Fental volunteers.

"Care to enlighten us?" Aristotle asks.

Atany starts laughing softly.

"It appears that the corridor leading from the main cavern to the chamber collapsed. Readings indicate the collapse happened some eighty hundred and fifty years ago."

"That explains why no one has ever found it," Atany says. She thinks a second, then says, "Any chance we can get it?"

"There's always a chance," Fental answers with just a touch of friendly sarcasm. "Give me a minute and I'll let you know if we can get to it." She buries her face in the monitor as she keys in commands.

Nearly a minute passes as she continues to input and analyze data.

"Okay," Fental begins. "The entrance to the cavern has also collapsed, so there is no direct access to the surface. The dense composition of the rock will not allow us to beam very far in. It appears we'll have to walk about three kilometers to the collapsed section." She turns to face the captain. "Are you up for a hike?"

"Are you kidding?" Atany replies. "I love hiking. How about you?"

"I'm ready," she answers. "Let's do this."

The two women stand as Professor Hawking walks to them.

"Have lieutenant Abaddon meet us in the transporter room," Atany tells communications officer Reuben as the three head into the turbolift.

Abaddon enters the transporter room as the two women are checking their field equipment. Hawking is standing by the transporter controls with the transporter chief.

"What's up, Captain?" he asks as he nods hello to everyone in the room.

"Get your field gear, Lieutenant," the captain orders as she turns to the transporter chief to verify the coordinates.

Abaddon heads to the locker on the other side of the room. He looks over at Fental.

"We're going hiking in some caves," she tells him with a smile.

"Oh joy," he replies. He steps onto the platform after getting his gear, and the four fade away in blue sparkles.

The four materialize in darkness so thick one cannot see their own hand at the tip of their nose. There is a brief moment of silence.

"Be careful when you turn your lights on," warns Hawking. "The moment the light goes on is—aarrgghh!" He slams his eyes closed tightly as he raises his hands for extra coverage. After a breath to calm down, he finishes, "When your eyes are the most sensitive."

"Sorry about that, Professor," Abaddon says apologetically, angling his light away from Hawking's face.

The others take out their lights and look around the cavern. Dutona opens her tricorder and scans the area. She turns, aiming her light several meters ahead.

"This way," she says as she raises her light's beam farther out until a wall comes into view. In that wall is an opening leading to a cave that goes farther than her light can reach. The four start walking, Dutona in the lead.

Forty minutes later, the four are standing in front of a wall of crumbled rock, the pieces so big and in place so long they look like a natural formation. Fental activates her tricorder and scans the area.

"The signal is coming from five meters beyond this wall. This wall is just over two meters thick," she reports.

Abaddon draws his phaser and aims at the base of the hidden opening.

"I wouldn't do that," Fental says with a slight hint of excitement.

"Why not?" Atany interjects.

"The rock above is unstable for half a kilometer up. If we blast through, the loose rock from above will come down and we will be dead," Fental explains matter-of-factly.

"Abaddon," the captain continues to interject, "don't do that, please."

"Absolutely not," he agrees.

"Any ideas?" Atany asks Fental.

"Standby," she answers as she scans both sides of the opening. It takes a number of seconds for her to finish. She focuses her attention at a spot on the wall several meters to the right. She points to the spot.

"Fire two phasers at that spot," she instructs. "Set them to level 6 and maintain fire for eight seconds. That will melt the rock enough to create a large enough opening to the chamber."

"Then let's do this," the captain says. "Abaddon, you're with me." The two draw their phasers and adjust the settings as they walk near the spot indicated by Fental. They aim and fire.

After three seconds, the rock starts glowing in a two-meter-diameter circle. A few more seconds and the rock within the circle starts to vaporize from the nine thousand degrees produced by both phasers.

After eight seconds, they stop firing. They have to wait another five seconds for the rock to cool down. The four enter the newly formed tunnel cautiously.

They enter the sealed-off section of the cave. Dutona scans the room and focuses on a spot about ten meters from where they entered. The four flashlight beams converge on the spot Dutona indicates, and they all see a wall full of glyphs, unseen by anyone for over eight centuries. A huge smile spreads across Professor Hawking's face.

The captain turns to him. "Are these Forzak?" she asks.

"I don't know. Give me a second," he answers as he runs his finger across several rows of glyphs, hoping to find familiar symbols. Midway through the third row, his eyes widen and his smile envelopes his face. He laughs softly but uncontrollably.

"Yes, Captain. Yes, they are," he finally answers as he pulls out his padd and starts recording images of all the glyphs in a systematic, orderly fashion, forever preserving the integrity of the find before continuing their investigation.

While Hawking is recording, Dutona attempts to locate the source of the signal. It only takes her a few seconds.

"Captain," she says, her voice giving away her excitement. "The source of the signal is emanating from one meter beneath this rubble."

"Okay, then," Atany starts, "Fental, Abaddon, set your lights up and let's get this shit cleared." She sets her flashlight on a rock and starts clearing away rocks. The two acknowledge her order and follow suit.

It takes about ten minutes for the three to clear away enough debris to see an ornamental box against the wall. Professor Hawking sees the box and, as soon as he finishes recording the glyphs, joins in the digging.

It takes another fifteen minutes with the four working to clear the rest of the debris from the artifact. They all look at the site in awe. After several long moments of silence, Professor Hawking breaks the silence.

"Captain, look at the leg of the table," he says, awestruck. "Does it look familiar?"

"The artifact. Holy shit!"

Fental and Abaddon are similarly awestruck. Aristotle takes out his padd and starts recording every detail. He finishes in five minutes.

"We need to get this back to the ship right now." A sense of urgency thick in his voice.

"Aren't you going to open it?" Abaddon asks.

"Oh, hell no," is his reply. "Not until I can study these glyphs. You must understand, after fifteen years of studying stories from antiquity and finding a glyph here and a passage there, to finally hold not just a piece, but also a fully intact artifact, this is a dream come true to the highest order," emotion overwhelming him. "I can only open this in a controlled environment. There can be no other way."

"Copy that, Professor," he responds. "So I guess we have to carry these things back to the transport coordinates?"

"Copy that, Lieutenant," Aristotle mocks back jokingly. The two men pick up the box. The two women pick up the table.

"It's not as heavy as it looks," Abaddon comments as they leave the chamber, prizes in hands.

An hour later finds Captain Atany and Lieutenant Fental on the bridge and Professor Hawking in a lab, converted from a cargo bay, while Lieutenant Abaddon is in the mess hall.

"Lieutenant Merah, set a course to the coordinates that Fental locked in before we left, and give me an ETA at warp two."

"Aye, Captain," he responds as he manipulates the controls to her will. He checks his display panel and answers, "ETA two point six hours."

Forty-five minutes pass when Lieutenant Reuben, at the communications station, breaks the silence.

"Captain, Professor Hawking would like to see you in his lab right away."

"Tell him I'm on my way." She gets up and heads for the turbolift. "Fental, you're with me."

Dutona gets up and follows.

"Come in," Hawking responds to the door chime. The door opens, and the two women enter the room.

"Ah, ladies. Come. Sit." He smiles, and the two women comply.

"What's up, Professor?" Fental asks.

"Two things, actually," he starts. "I have several ideas, but I need to speak to my colleagues on Brantax Three. Is that possible?"

"Of course," Fental answers. "I just need to know the frequency they are using."

"Channel zeta eight, two, zero, Lieutenant," he offers. Fental keys in commands on the computer terminal and after a few seconds, "Channel open and available," Fental says.

"Thank you, Lieutenant. After I talk to Shawn, Captain, I'll have much more information for you. How much longer before we arrive at the asteroid?"

"About twenty minutes."

"Excellent. I only need about fifteen, so if you two want to wait, that would be cool."

"We'll be in the mess hall when you're ready, Professor," Atany says. The two women stand and leave as Hawking turns to the computer console.

Fifteen minutes go by. Atany and Fental are finishing their coffee.

"Bridge to the captain," comes over the ship's PA system.

Atany turns to the console to her right and hits a control. "Atany here," she says.

"Captain, Professor Hawking would like to see you."

"We're on our way." The two get up and leave the mess hall.

"Come in! Come in!" Hawking screams with excitement.

"What's up, Professor?" the captain asks with a smile as the women enter the room.

He looks up at them with a huge smile. "Shawn and I have deciphered many more of the glyphs. And even though we've just scraped the tip of the iceberg, so to speak, the puzzle is coming together." He pauses to catch his breath. "The newly deciphered glyphs in the caves on Brantax Three and Zareth make reference to a device that will generate a type of vortex, something like a wormhole inside of a black hole. On the other side of the vortex, we will find the Forzak homeworld."

"Does it tell where we can find that device?" Atany asks intently.

"Shawn and I have deciphered another section that tells that the device was disassembled into six pieces and spread across the region."

"What about the box and table?" Dutona asks, equally intent.

"I sent images from those items to Shawn. He'll work on those with the rest of the team."

"What are we going to do until we get their report?" comes from the science officer, still entranced, as is the captain.

"Well, since the artifact you initially gave me is actually a leg off the table, I think it is safe to assume that there was another box on that asteroid. If it's not there, we may still find some other clues."

"Well, we'll be at the asteroid in about forty minutes," Fental says.

"That's right." Atany remembers. "Fental, return to the bridge and let me know when we get there."

"Will do," she says as she gets up and leaves.

Atany gets up from the chair and walks over to Hawking, sitting down on the sofa beside him, her full thigh firmly in contact with his. He looks up from his computer monitor to her leg then to her face. His smile widens when he sees she is smiling at him.

"How long do you think it will take to decipher all the glyphs?" The nervousness in her voice exposes the fact that she's looking for a reason to get close. Their eyes are affixed for what seems to be a long time as he desperately tries to look away from her gaze.

"I'm sorry," he says as he looks back at the monitor. "But you are so fucking gorgeous." He finishes with a slight nervous laugh.

"Thank you," she says shyly, looking away for a long second.

"You know I've felt an attraction since the first time we met?" she half asks as her eyes meet his again. They draw in close, sharing a slow, gentle kiss that slowly gets more intense. As they press their lips harder together, Atany starts to moan softly, enticingly.

Their lips separate, and Aristotle runs the tip of his tongue softly, slowly down Atany's neck. He runs his tongue back up her neck. When he reaches her ear, he draws her lobe into his mouth and gently sucks on it. Her arms squeeze him tighter as she moans louder.

He brushes his lips softly along her cheek until they find their way to her awaiting lips. They start kissing with a passion neither had felt in a long time. Her moans get even louder when he grabs her hair, pulling firmly but gently, arching her head back, enabling their kiss to be deeper and their tongues to dance together. They hug tightly after they break from their second long kiss.

"My gods," he whispers in her ear then takes in a long, deep breath through his nose. "The smell of your body is so intoxicating." His senses swimming in his head.

Atany lets out a long moan of ecstasy. "Thank you" slides from her lips with the last of her breath.

"Give me your tongue," he whispers to her.

Atany extends her tongue during their next kiss. Aristotle wraps his lips around it at its tip and slowly draws it into his mouth as far as he can. He slides her tongue out to its tip then slowly takes it in again. After several more times, Atany moans intensely as she starts rubbing her legs together, trying to ease the fire forming inside her.

Beep . . . beep . . . beep, breaks the silence and the mood.

"What is it?" Atany asks while trying to catch her breath, her voice sounding slightly crass.

"We'll be at the coordinates in about ten."

"Excellent. We'll be right up."

"We'll pick this up later," she says to Hawking. She gives him a kiss as she starts to stand. "Let's go."

"You can count on it," he replies with a smile as he stands.

"Status report," Atany orders as she takes her seat on the bridge, Hawking falling in to her left.

"We will be at the coordinates in two minutes," Fental reports.

"On main viewer," the captain requests, and the image of an empty void appears on the viewscreen. Atany looks slightly confused.

"Dutona," she starts with sarcastic annoyance. "Where's the damned asteroid?"

"I don't know, Captain," she answers confusedly. "Give me a minute." The bridge is silent for several long minutes.

"Ah, there it is. Come to heading three, one, two mark four, six."

Helm answers and sets a course.

"ETA is twelve minutes," Lieutenant Merah answers.

"Apparently, I didn't take into account that the damn thing is moving, and since we had no frame of reference for trajectory, I had to find it," Fental explains.

"Fair enough," Atany says.

"Captain," Lieutenant Korah, at tactical, says, breaking the silence after five minutes. "I'm picking up an intermittent signal on the very edge of sensor range."

"What do you make of it?"

"It's a ship. Bearing one, eight, zero mark one, seven, seven. It's staying just outside of range, shadowing us."

"Can you make out who it is?"

"No. Not at this distance," is the last thing said for almost a minute.

"I've got it! Hold on, Professor," she says quickly as she sits up straighter. "We're not giving these pricks a chance." She takes a breath. "Helm, lay in a course to put us, let's say, a hundred thousand kilometers behind that ship."

Fental looks confused.

"Course plotted and locked in."

"Engineering," Atany says into her armrest panel. "Activate the space-fold drive. Course is already locked in."

"Aye, Captain," echoes on the bridge. Five seconds later, the familiar dizzying star pattern appears on the viewscreen, and in an instant, the *Heaven* is behind the unknown ship.

"Now, who the hell are they?" the captain asks as she shakes off the space-fold drive effect, as do Fental and Hawking.

"It's the Rillians again, Captain," Lieutenant Korah replies.

"Really?" she asks rhetorically. "I guess they didn't learn their lesson the first time around." She spins her seat to face Korah.

"Lock phasers on target. Blow those fuckers out of my sky," she orders sternly as she spins back to face the screen.

The fluorescent blue phaser beams find the Rillian ship, and after a few seconds, the ship explodes into vaporous dust.

"Get us to that asteroid now, please," Atany says firmly.

"ETA eight minutes," Helmsman Merah replies.

"No!" Atany barks. "Get us there now! Warp five!" She sits back.

"Aye, Captain. ETA now fifteen seconds."

"That's better. Fental, find me that damn signal, ASAP!"

"On it, Captain." She turns and buries her face in the scanner.

The asteroid comes into view after about seven seconds. The ship slows as it approaches orbit.

"Fental," the captain asks, "have you located that signal yet?"

"Not yet, Captain. It is a very large asteroid."

The ship comes along the starboard side of the icy rock. At two-thirds impulse, it takes the *Heaven* a full four minutes to get to the front of the massive object.

The *Heaven* pulls ahead of the asteroid and cuts across the front. It takes another four minutes to scan the port side.

"Anything?"

"Not yet, Captain."

"Where the fuck is the other piece?"

"I can't answer that until I'm done scanning."

"We just went around the whole thing."

"The asteroid does have a sizable width, Captain. Our scanners are set on narrow beam."

"I see your point, Fental. Helm, take us on top of this thing."

The ship goes vertical and, after a few seconds, rolls port and finds itself seventy-five meters above the surface, thanks to Lieutenant Merah's expert piloting skills. The *Heaven* makes its way to the front of the asteroid.

"I've got the signal," Fental says with an element of surprise in her voice. Later, she would recall that she felt relief.

"Finally! Good job. Can it be transported up?"

"Stand by."

Puzzlement appears on the captain's face.

"It appears by these readings that there had been a disturbance in the cavern where the signal is emanating from," Fental reports. She continues analyzing the data for several minutes.

"It appears the box is intact but the table is in three pieces, two legs and the top. We have one leg on board already. That leaves one leg unaccounted for."

"And any glyphs that might be on the walls," Hawking adds.

"We can fix that," Korah volunteers after several minutes.

"Explain," Atany says.

"As far as the glyphs are concerned, ma'am, we can mount a camera on top of a portable floodlight rigged with a remote-controlled turret. We can beam it into the cavern and record any glyphs remotely."

"That's a fucking brilliant idea," she commends. "How long will it take you to set up the rig?"

"About twenty minutes."

"Then get to it," she instructs.

"Aye, ma'am," he says as he leaves the bridge.

"Rueben," the captain says to the communications officer. "Have the transporter room beam the artifacts from the cavern directly into the cargo bay with the other artifacts."

"Yes, Captain," he says as he carries out her orders.

"Right on. Now, Professor, let's go see your new toys," Atany says as she stands. "Fental, let's go." The three get on the turbolift.

The doors to Hawking's makeshift lab open, and the three walk in. At the far end of the room, near the box and table retrieved from Zareth, is another box and table. Unlike the pristine artifacts, the new box is slightly beaten and the table is in multiple pieces. Despite the damage, the two sets of artifacts are exactly the same dimensions. The only discernable difference is the glyphs carved into them. The three approach, and Aristotle starts to examine them, taking out his padd and recording each and every glyph. He sends them off to Shawn for analysis.

"Can I have a few hours to confer with Shawn and another colleague about our discoveries?"

"Of course, Professor. We have other duties to attend to in the meantime. Call the bridge when you have news." The two women leave.

On the bridge, all is running smoothly. Level one diagnostics on all systems shows everything is at one hundred percent. Fental and Atany are reviewing the images of the glyphs on the artifact since they returned to the bridge, in hopes of assisting the professor in finding out where they need to go next. After three and a half hours, both women are showing signs of fatigue. The images of the glyphs in the cave, taken by Korah remotely, are archived with the rest but offer little help in the work they are doing. The doors to the turbolift open.

"Captain," he proclaims. "I have a conundrum. I could really use Fental's expertise, as well as your help, of course."

"Sure, Professor. What's up?" she answers.

"I was conferring with Professor Arad Zor."

"The astrophysicist?" Dutona interrupts.

"Yes. Do you know him?"

"Just by reputation."

"Well, anyway, I was conferring with Zor and Shawn. We all agree that the Forzak used two reference points to plotting courses through space. We also found that the glyphs on the table are the spatial graphing coordinates."

Both women look confused, as do the rest of the bridge crew. Hawking looks around after noticing the looks on the captain and science officer and notices that same look on everyone else.

"That's to say . . ." he starts as he takes the padd from the young yeoman standing on the side of him. He keys in several somewhat lengthy commands. When he finishes, the main viewscreen turns white. He uses his finger as a stylus on the padd, and what he draws shows on the viewscreen. He draws two circles and puts a random dot on both. "The numbers on the table itself give us the location we need to be at on the planet." He draws a line from each dot within the circle. They intersect several centimeters away. "The numbers on the legs tell us at what degrees to aim at. When we simulate a beam, calculated this way, from two locations, where they intersect will be the location of the next artifact, and so on."

Everyone on the bridge show a sign of relief at how easy it is to understand. Dutona looks at Hawking with wide-eyed amazement.

"How did you hack into the viewscreen with that padd?" Her voice mirroring her look.

"Before I got my degrees in archeology and history, I received advanced degrees in computer software engineering and design. Some of my work went into designing these systems," he answers softly, somewhat humbly. He deactivates the padd, and the main viewscreen returns to star pattern outside of the ship.

"No shit?" she half asks, half replies.

"No shit," he retorts with a smile.

She smiles back. "What's your conundrum, Professor?" Atany asks.

"When we feed the data into the computer, the resulting simulation makes absolutely no sense. I would like Fental to double-check the calculations to back sure the math is sound."

"I already know your error, Professor," she says confidently.

"What?" A look of confusion crosses his face. "How the fuck can you know what I did wrong without even looking?" he asks.

"It's in the script," she answers matter-of-factly. Everyone on the bridge starts laughing out loud.

"You've been waiting a long time to use that line, haven't you?" Atany asks in between laughs.

"Shit yeah," she replies. "But seriously, I did the same thing a short time ago. I'm going to say you didn't take into account that the multiverse is expanding. You need to calculate the trajectories of all celestial objects and trace them backward for a millennium or so and try again."

"Holy fuck," he says with embarrassment all over his face and in his voice. "I feel like such a fucking idiot."

"No worries, Professor," Atany consoles with a smile. "Your secret is safe with us."

"Well then," he says, feeling slightly better. "While I run new simulations, can we make our way to Brantax Three?"

"Sure. Why?" she asks.

"So far we have artifacts in places where there are symbols on the walls."

The captain and science officer nod in agreement.

"Brantax Three has symbols on the walls, but we've yet to find the artifact. My team is working to solve that problem as we speak."

The glow over enlightenment shines across the faces of the two women.

"Helm, lay in a course to Brantax Three. Warp four."

I will be running simulations to try to find the next one," Hawking says as he leaves the bridge.

"ETA four hours, thirty-five minutes," Merah says.

"I'll be in my quarters if you need me," Atany says aloud to everyone as she heads toward the turbolift and to her quarters.

"Captain," the disembodied voice snaps her out of a dream, a dream she desperately wanted to get back to.

"Captain." Now she's more alert.

"What is it, Fental?" she asks sluggishly.

"Ten minutes to Brantax Three."

"Very good. I'll be there in seven." Atany straightens out her appearance in the mirror. She wakes up with a cup of strong coffee then heads to the bridge. She arrives a few minutes ahead of schedule. She silently takes her seat.

"Open a channel to Professor Hawking's colleagues."

"Channel open," Roeton replies.

"This is Captain Dinema Atany of the alliance starship *Heaven*."

"Hello, Captain." A familiar face appears on the screen.

"Shawn, is it?"

"Yes, Captain."

"You know why I'm contacting you, yes?"

"Yes. We've been able to scan two hundred thousand square kilometers around the dig site, but we've come up empty-handed."

"Have you told Hawking yet?"

"Yes. About twenty minutes ago. He acknowledged my report, said he was working on something and would get back to me."

"Thank you, Shawn. I'll contact you shortly. *Heaven* out." The viewscreen switched to Brantax Three from orbit. Atany turns and enters the turbolift.

Atany enters the lab and, without a word, walks up to Hawking. He turns around when he hears her approaching. Silently, she looks into his eyes and pulls him in for a long, sensual kiss, pressing her lips passionately against his. She darts her tongue playfully against his.

Aristotle smells the scent of her body, and his senses start swimming in his head faster and stronger than any drink or drug he had ever tried. He knew now that she is also much more addictive than any drink or drug.

After the kiss, she places her hands on the sides of his head, as if to hold him steady. "Good morning," she says with a voice full of excitement and a huge beautiful smile as she looks into his eyes. The smile slowly fades as she pulls him in for another kiss. His knees start to buckle, and his head spins deeper and faster into the vortex that is Dinema Atany. Waves of desire envelop his entire being.

"What's going on, Ari?" Atany asks when she pulls away from the second kiss. She looks into his eyes again, her glowing smile returns. "I've been thinking about that since I've been up," she tells him.

"Wow," he replies, almost fully out of breath. "So have I." He smiles back. "So have I." He continues after a second, "I was going to call you in a few minutes, but I'm glad you came down here." His look becoming slightly more serious.

"Is something wrong?" she asks with concern.

"Just a bit confused," he starts. "Maybe I've been looking at these glyphs for too long."

"What is it?"

"Not having an artifact near the cavern where my team is working has me perplexed. Since we've found two under similar circumstances, I can't figure out what happened to this one."

"Maybe someone found it already," Atany proposes.

"If someone would have found it, I'm sure they wouldn't have kept it a secret."

"Point taken," she replies as the chirp of the communications panel fills the room.

"Ah, excuse me, Captain. That's Shawn," he says as he walks to the console. "Any luck, Shawn?"

"Not at all, Ari," the voice answers. "We've kicked it around and can't find any correlation. Nothing makes any sense."

"Well, keep trying and if anything else—"

"I know, I know, Ari," Shawn interrupts. "If we find anything, I'll let you know. Good luck, Ari."

"Thank you, Shawn. We'll talk soon." He heads back to Atany. "Damn," he says with some disappointment.

"What else is wrong?"

"Glyphs I found on the table from the asteroid. We can't seem to determine their significance."

"What glyphs?" she asks, the spark of curiosity in her eye.

"There is a glyph at the top of the leg we think is the word *us*. Under it is the number two. Under that is what we think is *thing* or *item*, we're not sure. Then, under that is *last*."

"*Us, two, thing, last*? That's your newest conundrum?"

"Yes. None of my colleagues have a clue, I'm stumped, it's messed up."

Atany looks at the four words on the padd for a few silent minutes. Her face twists with confusion as her eyes lift to Hawking.

"It would be too easy if the two were a three," she comments.

"What do you mean?"

"Well, look," she says as she points to the first word. "*Us* could mean the Forzak. If the two were a three, it could be Brantax Three. Then the third word could be *piece*, as in piece of the device."

"Then *last* could be . . . the last planet in the system?" he interjects.

"Exactly," Atany confirms. "And the last planet in the system is Brantax Eleven. Let's get to the bridge." They stand and leave. She continues in the hall. "Now what would be the significance of the two?"

"I don't know," Hawking admits. "Maybe it's the Forzak version of a typo." The turbolift doors open to the bridge. They step out laughing.

Atany sits in her seat as Hawking goes over to the secondary science station, located to Fental's left, to run spatial trajectory simulations.

"Holy fuck," Atany says to herself yet loud enough for all to hear. "Fental, show me the entire Brantax system's trajectory back-tracked a millennium, at high speed."

"Yes, Captain," she says and complies.

"Display it on the main viewer when ready," she adds.

It took about a minute before the viewscreen changes and it becomes a simulation of the Brantax system. In the upper right corner of the screen is the display of the current standard stardate.

The planets on the screen stop moving. They start orbiting backward, slowly at first, gaining speed every second. In thirty seconds, a full one hundred years pass by.

"What's on your mind, Captain?" Hawking asks.

"It's a far out guess, but what if Brantax Three was Brantax Two a thousand years ago?"

"Very interesting," he says.

At the six hundred year mark, all is the same; at seven hundred, the same. At eight hundred, thirteen years past, Brantax two nearly collides with Brantax Three then shoots out of orbit.

"Stop right there!" Atany shouts as she points to the screen. Fental complies, and the simulation stops and then proceeds forward at a faster pace. As the simulation progresses, they see a rogue planet enter the Brantax system. Rather than colliding with Brantax Two, it fell into the larger planet's gravitation field and spun into an orbit between Brantax Two and the sun. As it settles into its new orbit, the rogue planet becomes Brantax Two, and Two becomes Three.

"Fuckin' aayy!" Fental says somewhat loudly.

"Very good, Captain," compliments Hawking. "Very impressive, but there goes my typo theory." He laughs.

"Well, now we know what they meant by two." She's laughing also.

"Helm, set a course for Brantax Eleven. Best possible speed."

"Course laid in. ETA four minutes," Lieutenant Levi answers.

"Lieutenant Sacar, get ready to start scanning as soon as we get into range."

"Where do we start, Captain?" Sacar asks.

Atany looks at Hawking. "Since we can assume the artifact has not been discovered yet, we need to find a place that has not been fully explored. I think that's the only way it would not have been found."

A minute goes by. All is quiet, everyone just waiting for the scanners to find their initial starting point.

"Captain," Fental breaks the momentary silence. "May I make a suggestion?"

"Of course. What's up?"

"As we've been doing for the regional spatial trajectory simulations, I contacted the central government's office of the interior and received the data from their geological division. I've done comparative studies of the surface and found a discrepancy that could possibly be a starting point."

"Fill us in, please," comes from the captain.

"Five centuries ago, there was a valley that is now an inland sea. I've done scans and found a series of underground caverns."

"Can you scan for our elusive signal?"

"Not until we are much closer. The density of the water will block the transmission significantly."

"Levi, get us to the coordinates of that water and get us close enough for Fental to scan. And get us there now."

"With these coordinates, ETA is three minutes."

The ship enters orbit close to the coordinates. Levi takes the ship close enough for Fental to start scanning.

"I think I may have something, Captain," Dutona says after eight minutes. "An intermittent signal is coming from near the northern shore. Coordinates transferred to helm."

"Okay, Levi, get us there and bring us into the upper atmosphere."

"There, Captain. Orbit stationary at one hundred fifty kilometers."

"What's up, Dutona?"

"There we go," she answers. "I can get a transporter lock on the artifact, but because of the water, we will not be able to send in a remote camera to look for glyphs."

"I think we can record the location, and if we need, we can deal with that when necessary. Just recover the artifact for now."

"All right. Fental, make sure that the artifact gets into Hawking's lab." She gets up. "Hawking, Fental, you're with me." They leave the bridge.

The three enter the lab to find three artifacts. There is a beeping sound permeating the air. As they get closer to the artifacts, they realize the beeping is coming from the computer console.

"Excellent!" Hawking says. "The simulations are complete." He walks over to the terminal. "We have a location. I'll lock in the coordinates and run the trajectory forward. We'll have the current location in a few minutes."

The two women admire the artifacts as Hawking takes images of the glyphs while the computer runs the simulation. It takes about two minutes for the computer to start beeping.

"We have the location of the next artifact."

"Excellent," Atany says. "Where is it?"

"Ah, fuck," he answers after he looks on the monitor.

"What is it?" Dutona asks.

"According to these coordinates, it is dead smack in the middle of the Danarus asteroid field."

"Great," the captain answers back. "Now we have to go play chicken with some rocks, some really big rocks." They laugh lightly.

"Do you know how long it will take us to get there?" he asks.

"Not at the moment. I'll let you know when we get back to the bridge."

"That'll work. While we are on route to the asteroid field, I will work on the glyphs on the boxes after I get the info from the table."

"Very good, Professor. We will be on the bridge. We'll call you when we get there."

When the two women leave the room, Hawking starts working on deciphering the table glyphs.

The doors to the bridge open. Atany and Fental step onto the command deck. The captain takes her seat while the science officer takes hers.

"Levi, set a course for the Danarus asteroid field. Warp six."

"Yes, Captain." He types commands. "Course plotted and laid in. ETA is thirteen point five hours."

"Copy that. Get us there," she says. "Fental, inform Professor Hawking of our ETA."

"Yes, Captain," Fental says and does.

Atany stands and walks to the turbolift. She stops just before activating the doors. She turns her head.

"I will be in my quarters if needed," she says and steps onto the turbolift and heads off to bed.

Chapter 3

Captain's log, stardate 29987.12. We are three point five hours away from the Danarus asteroid field to search for another of the Forzak artifacts. With the assistance of Professor Hawking and old-fashioned shit luck, we have already acquired three artifacts. In time, we hope to learn their secrets. The Rillians attempted to interfere twice. They will not be interfering again.

Atany steps onto the bridge and takes her seat. Her wide eyes and smile give away her well-rested demeanor. A yeoman comes over with the daily reports. She looks at the reports and approves them. She sits back in her seat.

The ship suddenly rocks as consoles around the bridge explode from power surges. On the screen, the star pattern becomes static, indicating the ship has dropped out of warp. The computer automatically sounds the red-alert klaxon as the bridge is bathed in red light.

"What the fuck is going on?" Atany screams in surprise.

"Checking, Captain!" Fental shouts over the klaxon.

"Damage control reports hull breach on deck three. Starboard, aft," says Lieutenant Sacar. "Forcefields are in place and holding. Two crewmen unaccounted for."

"Scanners showing a ship on our port side," Fental reports. "Sensors show it is Chandrakan."

"Aft shield generator hit!" Lieutenant Levi shouts. "Other generators compensating but shields at seventy-three percent."

"Come to a heading of one, six, five mark one, six, zero. Warp two for thirty seconds then change course to one, eight, zero mark two, zero, five and open fire with everything we have."

"Yes, Captain," comes from all on the bridge. The ship glides around to the captain's commands and, in less than a minute, is head on with the Chandrakan battle cruiser.

As the *Heaven* slowly approaches the formidable vessel, it rocks again from an explosion. Several seconds pass as power leaks from the shorted-out panels on some of the auxiliary controls.

"Sensors show two more Chandrakan ships aft!" shouts Lieutenant Sacar as he adjusts controls to compensate for the damaged circuits.

"Commander Asher!" Atany shouts into her communications console.

"Yes, Captain," his voice echoes.

"Fire up the spacefold drive. Now!"

"Will do."

"Lieutenant Levi! Plot the most direct . . ." The ship rocks again from the Chandrakan weapons. The captain continues, "Course so we are one hundred thousand kilometers behind those two ships."

"Course plotted and laid in," he answers after a few long seconds.

"Engage. Now!" she orders.

The ship moves toward the vessel in front of them. The spacefold drive kicks in a half a second before the ship makes its first maneuver.

In the blink of an eye, the *Heaven* is in the position the captain ordered.

On the viewscreen, the three Chandrakan ships move away from the *Heaven*, following the trajectory they think Atany and crew went.

"Now surprise is on our side," Atany says firmly. She looks around as she catches her breath. It takes about five seconds for all the crew on the bridge to stabilize the power surges and electrical fires that existed after their escape. After a few more seconds, Atany continues her plan.

"Sacar, lock a fill spread of torpedoes on the port side ship."

"Ready, Captain."

"Levi, set heading three, four, three mark zero. Warp two. Go."

Without a word, he complies, and the ship shouts off, but only for a few seconds. All is quiet, tense.

"Full impulse. Now," she says, looking at Levi. The ship slows to find it several hundred kilometers from the two ships closest together.

"Fire torpedoes. I don't care which ship you destroy, but destroy one of those fuckers."

The torpedoes fire, and the ship closest to the *Heaven* is vaporized in a series of torpedo detonations.

"Lock phasers on the second ship and fire," she says sternly.

The phasers fire. The second Chandrakan ship explodes as the beams from the phaser emitters tear through the ship's hull and into the fuel storage tanks.

Before the captain can comment on the efficiency of her crew, the ship is rocked by an explosion so intense that the lights throughout the ship flash on and off several times.

"Return fire. Now! As she comes to bear," she says. She takes a breath and continues, "Damage report."

"Warp core is offline. Impulse power is okay. Shields at forty-five percent. Phaser banks full, but all torpedo tubes are down. Repair time is estimated at six hours," comes from Roeton after several seconds.

"What's the status of the Chandrakan ship?"

"Their engines are damaged, but weapons are still online," Fental answers, then continues after a sensor sweep, "Their shields are full."

"Best speed to the Danarus asteroid field," she orders. She spins her chair to face Roeton. "Tell engineering to grab as many hands as they need, but I want the warp drive back online yesterday."

"On our way. ETA two days, sixteen hours and forty-four minutes," Levi reports.

"Engineering replies warp drive number one priority," Roeton tells the captain.

> *Captain's log. Supplemental. Warp drive is back online. Repair time, just over three hours. Shields and torpedo launchers are still under repair. Damage control reports another four hours before those systems are at 100 percent. All secondary systems are operational. The space-fold drive took serious damage. It is unknown whether we will be able to get it operational or have to pull into dry-dock for repairs. We are ten minutes away from the Danarus asteroid field. There is no sign of the Chandrakan battle cruiser that we encountered three and a half hours ago. With luck, we will be out of here in a matter of hours with the fourth component.*

"Bring us into the field from the farthest point starboard and start a grid pattern search," Atany tells Fental. "I'm going to find out if professor Hawking has gotten any further in the translations," she continues as she stands and heads toward the turbolift.

The captain enters Hawking's lab to find him facedown in his monitor and making notes on a padd beside the screen. He is so immersed in his work that he didn't hear her come in. She walks up behind him.

"Hello, Professor," she says with a springy lightness in her voice.

"Aahh!" Hawking screams. "What the fuck!" His arms flailing as the padd he is working on goes flying off the table and the monitor summersaults several times before smashing on the floor.

Atany jumps back with equal surprise. "Oh . . . I'm sorry, Professor."

"Well, that sucked," he says with a shutter in his voice. He takes a deep breath and continues, "You scared the shit out of me. Don't do that again." He takes another, deeper breath.

"Really, I'm sorry, Professor. I didn't mean to freak you out," she says as she picks the padd up from the floor. It is only now he sees the outfit she has changed into.

The skirt is ankle long and closely forming to her legs, with hip-high slits on both sides. From his position, Hawking sees her long, slender, bare legs. As his eyes glide up her firm thighs, the fabric of her skirt tightens and forms to her full, firm ass. Her blouse is even more provocative. His slacks start to feel tight.

Hawking picks up the computer monitor and sets it on the desk where it was. Atany hands Hawking his padd as the two sit on the sofa by the desk. They sit angled, facing each other, her legs crossed with her left leg across his thighs, the smooth skin of her firm, toned leg shining in the low light of the single lamp on the desk.

"How far along are you with the translations?" she asks softly. After staring at her leg for several seconds, he snaps himself back to reality and looks up at her face. The huge, beautiful smile reveals that she caught him admiring her. He stutters as he starts to speak.

"I ha-have figured out that the inscriptions on the tables are directions to two artifacts."

"That's it?"

"That's it," he answers.

She looks at him inquisitively.

"What is it?" he asks.

"I'm just wondering, why two artifacts?"

"Probably to ensure that all six components are found."

"Makes sense," she answers while Hawking scrolls through the contents on his padd. He stops at an image of the three tables, each table in its own column of four photos. "For now," she finishes.

"Look at these," he says as he leans in closer to show her the images. She reciprocates as her eyes rise up to his. They both look at the padd. "See now, the column on the left is from Brantax Eleven, the column in the center is from Zareth, and the right is from the rogue asteroid." He looks at her. "Here's where it gets complicated."

He smiles as he looks back at the padd and says sarcastically, "So please try to keep up."

She slaps his arm playfully as they laugh.

"The table from Brantax Eleven gives us two locations: one is Zareth, and the other is an unknown."

"Number five?" she asks excitedly.

"That's my thought." He then continues, "The one from Zareth gives us Brantax Eleven and the rogue asteroid. The one from the rogue asteroid gives us Brantax Eleven and the Danarus field."

"So when we get this one from Danarus, we can translate the two and maybe find the location of the sixth one as well."

"Absolutely," he says.

She giggles lightly as she takes his face in her hands and draws him in. They kiss long and hard. He puts his hand on the knee she has laid across his lap. While they kiss, he spreads his hand along her thigh and slowly, gently slides his hand up the length of her thigh, close enough to feel the heat from her body.

She moans lightly as their lips part. She catches her breath. "Squeeze my thigh," she says softly as she pulls him in for another kiss, sliding her tongue deep into his mouth. He squeezes her thigh firmly, and she moans deep and long, her body going slightly limp. The heat from between her legs intensifies around his hand. The smell of her body reaches his nose, and his head starts to swim. He moans loudly. She breaks the kiss and looks at him longingly.

"Is everything all right?" she asks.

"The smell of your body, my gods, you are so intoxicating."

"Thank you," she says softly and draws him in to continue kissing.

He slides his hand up her thigh just a bit more and gently caresses her clit. She moans more as she slides herself down. He slides a bit, and very soon they are lying down.

He slowly runs his tongue down her neck and, as he reaches the shoulder, slips the straps from her blouse off her shoulders and down to her elbows, exposing her supple breasts. The metal piercings in her nipples reflect in the lamplight. He slides his tongue between her breasts as his fingers tug gently on the metal studs in her nipples and her clit at the same time. She moans as her ass starts to grind under his hand.

Hawking runs his tongue farther down Atany's stomach and over the fabrics of her blouse and skirt. His lips brush lightly over her lower abdomen as he slides his body so her wet pussy is more readily available.

His tongue now lightly strokes her clit as his finger slides in and out of her hot, wet hole. So slowly she grinds her ass in a circular motion on the cushion.

Hawking continues to run his tongue all over her pussy, lips to clit then back to her lips again as his finger strokes the inside of her pussy.

"Oh, fuck," she says softly, in between gasps of breath. His tongue and finger now start to work in unison. After about fifteen minutes she says, "Oh gods, that feels so good." Her voice is so alluring and her face so beautiful during her orgasm that he could no longer stand it.

As he continues to lick and suck on Atany's hot, wet box, Hawking positions himself and takes his pants off, careful not to interrupt the rhythm he has going.

Now with his long, hard cock exposed, he shifts his body so his cock is in her face. He continues to suck on Atany's clit as he slides his finger back into her pussy, forcefully thrusting it in.

Atany moans as his finger slides deep inside her. Her moan continues with an air of impressiveness. She grabs his hard, throbbing cock in her hand and, as she starts to orgasm again, shoves it deep in her mouth, sliding in and out in a rhythm of her own. Hawking moans intensely; this makes her cum harder. His cock feels so large it should explode as he thinks of this beautiful woman with his cock in her mouth. They continue for what seems forever, Atany having several more orgasms.

Beep, beep, beep. The sound of the intercom panel breaks the mood of the room. The two bodies continue unaware.

Beep, beep, beep. "What the fuck?" Atany says with mock sobs. She rolls over and stands.

Beep, beep, beep. "Shut up!" she half shouts, partly angry as she slaps the intercom button.

"What is it?" she says with more composure.

"Bridge here, Captain." Fental's voice fills the room with a mechanical overtone. "Sorry to interrupt, but we have picked up the artifact signal."

"You have no idea," the captain says under her breath then continues, "I'll be there shortly. Out." She turns to Hawking as she raises her blouse back up to cover her breasts. She sees he is putting his pants on.

"Sorry, Professor. I'd *really* like to finish this but—"

"I know. Duty calls, for both of us," he says as she walks up to him and puts her arms around his neck. "I am so glad you are here." She smiles and gives him a long, passionate kiss. "I'll see you on the bridge in fifteen," she says as she leaves the room with a huge smile on her face.

The turbolift doors open, and the captain steps onto the bridge. Hawking and Fental are reviewing data at Fental's station when Atany walks over. The two lock eyes and smile, remembering the events of thirty minutes ago.

"What do we have?" she asks the two.

"The signal is coming from an asteroid at coordinates one, eight, one by seven, four, one by six, six, five. Fifty thousand kilometers at heading three, four, seven mark zero, one, zero," Fental reports.

"Bring us in, Levi, half impulse," Atany orders. "Slow and steady."

"Aye, Captain," he replies, and the ship starts to move slowly toward the signal. Levi flies the starship over and around asteroids of various shapes and sizes. Some made of iron, some of gold.

"Fental." The captain spins to face the science station. "Scan and catalogue these asteroids. Some of them look to be miners' paradises."

"Doing it now, Captain," she responds as she does as ordered.

The ship continues to glide eloquently around and under the asteroids, en route to the Forzak signal. What started at fifty thousand kilometers due to flying around seemed like seventy-five thousand. After twenty-five minutes, the asteroid emitting the signal appears on the main viewscreen as the ship comes over the horizon of a moon-size rock.

"Bring us within five kilometers, Levi."

"Yes, ma'am," he says and complies. The asteroid of interest slowly fills the viewscreen. It takes about three minutes.

"Five kilometers, Captain," Levi informs.

"The signal is coming from a cavern at the center of the aster-oid," Fental reports. "But—" she continues.

"Of course," the captain interrupts. "There has to be a *but*. What's the *but*, Dinema?" sarcasm thick in her voice and a smile across her face.

"But we have to bore a hole in the asteroid ten meters wide and sixty meters deep. It will take about two and a half minutes to com-plete," Fental says with some sarcasm of her own. She smiles back to the captain while the rest of the bridge crew giggled a bit.

"Well then," Atany continues, "make it so. Let's get that fucker up here." Ninety seconds later, a wide beam shoots from the *Heaven's* recalibrated phaser banks. The phasers fire for just under a minute then shut off automatically.

"Artifact is in the bay with the others. Decontamination will be complete in seven point two minutes," Fental reports after a few seconds.

"Well, Professor, let's go see the new artifact. Fental, you're with us." They head for the turbolift. Atany stops and turns to the crew.

"Levi, set a course to get us out of here. Once outside the field, just hang out until we get back up here."

He acknowledges her orders.

"Roeton"—she turns to the communications officer—"coordi-nate with damage control parties and get the rest of our repairs done."

"Will do, Captain" is the last thing Atany hears as the turbolift doors close.

The doors to the cargo bay / lab open, and the three see the new artifact encased in a softly humming forcefield. The computer on the desk is counting down loudly, being the second of the only two sounds in the room. The doors whoosh closed behind them.

"Two minutes, thirty seconds," the mechanical female computer voice announces coldly . . . then silence.

"Two minutes," she announces again.

"Good," Hawking finally speaks. "In two minutes, we'll see if I can figure out where to go next. He walks over to the computer and silences the countdown. He calls up commands on the monitor in preparation for the task at hand.

Two minutes later . . .

"Decontamination complete," the computer states.

"Okay," Hawking starts as he walks toward the artifact. "Fental, would you get logs of all the glyphs, please?"

"Sure thing, Professor," she replies as she grabs her equipment and proceeds quietly. Hawking starts a closer inspection across from where Fental is working. This artifact is much larger than the others, roughly two and a half times, yet sensors indicate it is much lighter than the other two. It seems oddly out of place.

"I wonder what's in here," Atany says out loud to herself.

"We can only guess right now," Hawking answers.

"It was a rhetorical question, Professor," she replies with a hint of embarrassment in her voice.

"I know," he says in a matter-of-fact sort of way. They both laugh for several seconds.

"All the glyphs have been logged and photographed," Fental says, breaking a momentary silence.

"Excellent!" Hawking says excitedly. "Put the images on a padd and bring them to the desk." He walks over and places the other padds on the desk beside the one Fental put down.

"Each padd contains glyphs from each of the artifacts, and the monitor has the glyphs from Brantax," Hawking explains. "Oh, Fental, can you get me an open channel to Brantax? I need to speak with Shawn as soon as possible."

"I can have you connected in just a minute," Fental says and then makes it happen. "Channel to Brantax open, Professor."

"Ari? Are you there? It's Shawn," the disembodied voice fills the room.

"Shawn, it's Hawking. How are you?"

"All is well here. What's up, Ari?"

"Shawn, we've found the fourth of the Forzak components."

"You're shitting me!" The sound of excited disbelief in his voice fills the room.

"No, Shawn, but I need your help right away."

"What do you need?"

"I'm going to send you a series of images from each of the artifacts. We're going to decipher the table glyphs to find the other two. We need you guys to decipher the glyphs on the boxes and verify what they say."

"As soon as I get the images downloaded, we will start the translation and get back to you when we have news," Shawn replies.

"Cool beans," Hawking answers. "Transmitting now," he says as he types in the commands. Several seconds go by.

"File downloads complete. I'll be in touch. Safe journeys, Ari."

"Good-bye, Shawn, and good luck. Hope to hear from you soon." The open channel goes silent.

"Now, ladies, what we need to do is find out where the next artifact is located. If you would give me a little time to focus, as soon as I have some translated, we can try to figure out where we need to go."

"Very good, Professor," Atany says as she stands. "Fental and I will be on the bridge. Call when you have news." The two women smile and exit the room. Atany blows Hawking a kiss as she walks out of the room. The professor buries his head in the monitor and padds.

"You like him?" Fental asks her captain. "Professor Hawking, I mean."

"I know who you mean, Fental. And to answer your question, yeah, I'm pretty smitten with him."

"I don't blame you. He is hot."

"Wicked hot."

"Yeah." They both start laughing as they enter the turbolift.

The turbolift doors open, and the women step onto the bridge. They both walk silently to their posts and sit, almost simultaneously. The bridge is silent. The air is still.

"Captain," Lieutenant Roeton breaks the silence that has lasted the better part of an hour. "Damage control reports all systems are back online. Space-fold drive is repairable but will take the better part of a day. We can go whenever you're ready."

"Go where?" she says softly. Like a wish made by a youngster on their birthday, the intercom in the captain's armrest starts beeping.

"Captain." Professor Hawking's voice permeates the air. "Can you come down to my lab, please?"

"What's up, Professor?" she responds.

"I have some of the glyphs translated."

"Say no more, Professor. I'm on my way." As she stands, she looks up. "Thank you, lords," she says softly, so softly that no one else heard.

"Fental, you're with me." The two step onto the turbolift.

Hawking looks up from the padds when he hears the door chime, knowing the captain is out in the hall.

"Come in, Captain, come in," he says loudly.

The door opens, and the two women enter the room.

"Ah, Lieutenant, welcome. How are you ladies doing?" he says with an odd grin on his face.

"About the same as an hour ago, but that will change depending on what you say in the next few minutes," Atany replies, in a hurry to get back to the mission.

"Okay then. I've deciphered a portion of the glyphs that may suggest a starting point, but it's in some kind of code. I don't understand the references," he starts, with some apology in his voice. "I was wondering if maybe you can give me your perspective on what they may mean. I don't want to send us to the wrong place."

"Show us what you've got," Fental responds, and Atany just smiles and nods in agreement. The three look at the padds on the table.

Hawking points to two of them. "I found similar references on these two, only they are inverted from each other. Above them are these series. The only thing I can make of those is . . . well, they translate to *foggy stars*, *three cycles complete*, and *eastern voyage south* on this one."

"And where's that one from?" Fental asks.

"That's from Brantax Eleven."

"Cool." Fental continues, "Give me a few minutes. I need to look something up." She turns to the computer on the table and starts keying in commands.

After about five minutes of silence, except for the sounds of the buttons on the keyboard being tapped, Atany speaks out. "What are you doing, Fental?" she asks with mock annoyance.

"I'm looking into the history of Brantax Eleven," she explains. "I'm looking to the ancient legends for those particular phrases."

"Let me guess," Atany starts. "You're a history buff?"

"Only Brantaxian history. My great-grandparents on my father's side came from Brantax Eleven."

"What about the glyphs from the other location?" The captain gets Hawking's attention. He turns to her with a look of slight surprise.

"Oh, yes, sorry, I'm slightly distracted," he answers.

"No worries, Professor. It's all good. Now, what do you have?"

"These glyphs are from the asteroid field." He picks up the padd and gets close to Atany. They are both looking at the padd in his hand.

"Now this glyph is a mirror image to the glyph from Brantax. Above it is this series. We have here, once again, *foggy stars*, but now we have what appears to be *eternally right in the night*. I'm lost."

"Are you sure the translations are correct?" Dinema asks somewhat sympathetically but with a smile.

"Positive. I double checked with Shawn, and he agrees. The translations are correct, but it just sounds like gibberish."

"Gods damned!" Fental screams. "It's not gibberish."

"What have you got, Fental?" the captain asks with a contagious excitement. They both walk over to her.

"Give me a few minutes to check one more thing." She keys in other commands and images from within the Danarus asteroid field come on the screen.

"Fental, what have you got?"

"One minute, Captain," she says without looking up.

"Fental, what's happening?" the captain asks again after a few more seconds, her patience wearing thin.

"I just need to verify my findings, so please be patient for a few more minutes. You wouldn't want faulty data, would you?"

"Point taken. I'm just somewhat itching to go."

"I have to find one particular image to verify my hypothesis."

Two minutes go by without anyone speaking a word. The keying of commands and the humming of the computer are the only noises in the room. Atany is showing excited anticipation.

"Found it!" Fental shouts.

"Found what?" Atany shouts almost as loud as Fental.

"The location of the fifth artifact!" she shouts back.

"Why are we shouting?" Dinema asks.

"I'm excited." Fental explains, "I just found the next artifact."

"Okay," Atany agrees. "Can we use our inside voices now?"

"Sorry," Fental says in a much lower tone.

Hawking stands there, laughing through the whole episode.

"Now, where is the next artifact, and how did you figure it out?" the captain asks.

"I'm the science officer. I'm supposed to know these things."

The three start laughing for several minutes.

"The next artifact is in the Rhinehart Nebula," Fental says when the laughter's over.

"How did you figure it out?" Hawking asks.

"The terms *foggy stars* and *three cycles complete*. Ancient Brantaxian stories describe the Rhinehart Nebula as foggy stars, and it is visible in the night sky for three full cycles of the moons. The *eastern voyage south* is the path across the night sky."

"That's awesome," Atany says, impressed with her first officer.

"Excellent," Hawking agrees. "But what about the other glyphs?"

"Ah, that's why I needed the images from the asteroid field," Fental replies. "Look at this." She motions them to look at the image on the monitor. "This image shows the asteroid field while the camera is aiming toward the center of the galaxy."

The three gaze at the image.

"What are we supposed to be looking at?" Hawking inquires.

"Think of the glyphs *foggy stars* and *eternally right in the night*. Look to the right of center. Do you see it?"

"Holy shit! I see it!" Hawking says astounded.

"What?" Atany says, still puzzled. "Oh fuck, I see it now. Right there." Atany points to a spot of blurred stars midway to the right side of the picture.

"Yep, the Rhinehart Nebula," Fental confirms.

Atany hits a button on the console. "Helm, how long to the Rhinehart Nebula, best speed?"

"Levi here, Captain, our best speed is warp seven point five and will take us twenty-seven point three hours."

"Very good. Do it. Get us there," Atany orders.

"Yes, Captain. We are out of here," Levi responds.

"Okay," Atany speaks to Fental and Hawking. "It'll take nearly a day to get there and a few hours sooner to fix the space-fold drive, so we have until we reach the nebula to find the last artifact's location and get the boxes translated."

"Of course. You're right, Captain," Hawking says. "I'm going to get on finding the last artifact."

"I'm heading to the bridge," Fental adds. "I'll see you there." She starts for the door.

"I'll be there in a few minutes," Atany volunteers. The door closes behind the science officer.

"Before you get back to work and I go to the bridge, Professor"—Dinema gets face-to-face and up close and personal with Hawking—"I want to kiss you. Is that okay?" she asks with her beautiful sly smile as she pulls him closer in. Her lips brush against his lightly as her tongue slides into his mouth.

Hawking's head starts to swim and his knees buckle. She pulls away slowly with the look of satisfaction on her face.

"That'll do for now," she says seductively.

"Yes, it will," Hawking agrees. "I'm going to get this work done. Come back down in, let's say, four hours, and we can have a bite to eat, a drink or two, maybe a little relaxation time."

"Maybe," she says, giggling. "But I'll be back in, let's say, four hours and we'll hang out." She heads toward the door, and as she exits the room, the last thing she sees is Hawking intensely glaring at the padds on the table.

Chapter 4

Captain's log, stardate 2999 5.33. We are en route to the Rhinehart Nebula in search of the fifth Forzak artifact. The space-fold drive will take nearly a full day to repair, just shy of the time it will take us to get to the nebula. Warp drive is repaired but is being held together with duct tape and paperclips. I hope we've seen the last of the Chandraka on this mission.

Atany takes her seat on the bridge to see the streaking star pattern, indicating that the ship is traveling at warp, on the main viewscreen.

The next two hours are boringly uneventful. Atany signs several status reports and keeps up on the space-fold drive repairs, and Fental continues to monitor sensor readings of the surrounding area as the ship races through space.

"Captain," tactical officer Korah shouts nervously. "I'm picking up a signal, one, three, five mark zero, nine, five. It is on an intercept course, traveling warp nine point two. Forty-five seconds until intercept."

"Fuck, we don't have time for this," Atany complains. "Helm, increase speed to warp eight."

"I'll try, Captain, but that could blow the whole system," Levi says.

"Understood," she answers as she hits a button on her armrest. "Benjamin," she shouts into the microphone, "make sure my engines don't blow apart!"

"I'll do the best I can but can't make any promises," the *Heaven*'s chief engineer answers back.

"I don't care if you have to shit on, piss on, or cum on those engines, but don't let them fail us now!" A slight hint of defiance in her voice.

"I won't let you down, Captain." The line goes dead.

"Helm, keep as much distance between us and that signal as possible, for as long as possible."

"I'm on it, Captain," Levi replies. "Warp eight." Atany turns to Korah. "Time to intercept?" she asks.

"Two point two-five minutes."

"Okay then," she answers to no one particular. "This isn't what I wanted, but so be it."

After a full minute, the stress level on the bridge is building to a nervous pitch as everyone is waiting for the captain to plot her next move. Atany is sitting in her seat, pondering the situation.

"Korah." She spins to him. "Do you know yet who that signal is?"

"Analyzing now," he replies and, after a brief second, says, "Sensors indicate the signal is Chandrakan. The same battle cruiser we encountered several hours ago. Apparently they have good engineers, very good engineers."

"All stations, yellow alert," she orders.

The klaxon sounds on every deck, and all crewmembers act accordingly, hurrying to their stations in anticipation of what's to come.

"Time to intercept forty-five seconds," Sacar informs.

"Go to red alert. Load photon torpedoes and charge phaser banks," Atany commands. "Shields to max."

The red alert klaxon blares, and the bridge is bathed in a red glow.

"Shields up, torpedo tubes loaded, and phasers at full charge," Korah volunteers. "Awaiting your orders, Captain."

Without warning, the ship suddenly rocks violently from side to side. Sparks fly from consoles all around the bridge as monitors blink out and come back to life.

"What the fuck was that?" Atany shouts in surprise. "Get damage control, on the double!"

"There is another vessel!" Dutona yells with confusion in her voice. "It is Rillian. It is swinging around for another—correction, there are two Rillian ships out there. One swinging around, and the other is making a pass now." The ship rocks again.

"Shit! Three to one, now that's not fair," Atany says aloud. "Swing us around one, three, five mark zero, zero, eight. Get us behind the Chandrakan ship."

"Aye, Captain," Korah answers as the ship leans to the right as it banks around.

"Damage control is on the scene," Lieutenant Reuben, at the communications console, informs the captain.

"We are flanking the Chandrakan battle cruiser," Korah states.

"Good, fire phasers and photons, full spread," Atany orders.

The Chandrakan ship, now on the main viewscreen, rocks as the barrage of firepower smashes into it.

"Their shields are down to five percent, minor buckling in their starboard hull," Fental reports.

"Very good," the captain acknowledges. "Get ready to—"

The ship rocks again. Conduits in the ceiling drop down, gases venting from their openings. Circuit panels explode in brightly colored sparks.

"Can we still fire?" Atany yells above the hissing of the venting gases.

"Yes, but power is low." She hears.

"Good, blast them again." She turns to Fental. "Where are the fucking Rillians?" her voice taut.

"They are two hundred and twenty kilometers aft. They're coming around for a pass, but we can take out the Chandraka before they get here," Fental reports.

"Blast those fuckers, Korah!" Atany screams, and on the viewscreen, the phaser beams hit their target and burn into it for what seems to be forever. After several long seconds, the area around the phaser impact starts to glow. Several seconds later, the Chandrakan ship vaporizes in a brilliant explosion.

"Full stop, zee axis minus ten thousand kilometers, now!" the captain yells with a little less urgency. The ship comes to a sudden stop and instantaneously drops straight down at near warp speed.

"How are my engines?" she screams into the armrest of her chair.

"They're still going strong, minor damage, no problem," Benjamin's voice booms.

"That's some good news," she says. "Weapons status?"

"Phasers and torpedoes fully functional," Korah answers.

"Even better," Atany says as she looks around the bridge, everything going in slow motion as she readies herself for the imminent threat ahead.

"Helm, warp five, heading zero, two, two mark zero, zero," Atany commands and continues, "In five seconds, bring us into a tight loop and straight down onto the lead ship."

The streaking star pattern of warp speed looks normal for a few seconds, then, suddenly, the stars start shooting in a downward motion on the screen. The view remains the same for about thirty seconds, then a tiny dot appears in the middle of the screen. As the seconds tick by, the dot grows larger and quickly becomes a Rillian attack ship. The image grows larger as they approach.

"Are we in range?" Atany asks.

"Will be," Korah starts, "in three, two, one . . ."

"Fire!" the captain yells excitedly.

"Volley away!" Korah shouts as, on the viewscreen, the weapons fire can be seen emerging from the bottom of screen to the target, two beams of fluorescent light and three torpedoes. The weapons make impact with the Rillian ship in a staggered progression. The phaser beams spread across the shields of the enemy ship. The first torpedo impacts on the shields as does the second one. The third torpedo explodes on the hull of the ship.

"Excellent," Atany says as she spins toward her science officer.

"Fental?" she calmly says.

"Their starboard shields are down, and they have a hull breach and are venting atmosphere," she answers without looking away from her monitor.

"Korah, lock on to that venting hull and blast them to hell."

"My pleasure, Captain," Korah replies happily as he fires, and once again the phasers and torpedoes hit in staggered form. The phaser beams burn into the hull and, seconds before the torpedoes detonate, explosions from inside the ship could be seen blasting out. Three more torpedoes explode on the hull, and the ship on the screen explodes into nothingness.

The bridge crew cheers, but their happiness is short-lived. The ship rocks violently once again, plunging the bridge into darkness. For several seconds, they all fumbled around in the dark. The darkness fell silent with the screams of terror.

Though hundreds of hours are spent by all alliance cadets in starship simulations of every conceivable contingency, including complete power loss during battle, when a ship losses all power and the darkness and coldness of space are only a few inches of metal plating away, utter darkness is the only thing that can be seen, the enemy is about to fire another round, and death is only seconds away, a person's mind has to be forced, even though so thoroughly trained, to stay alert and calm and not shut down in total fear, the fear of death. Atany is praying that her crew is all in the proper frame of mind. If even a handful of crewmembers fall into this blind panic, all will be lost and the *Heaven* will be obliterated.

It takes nearly four seconds before the battery power kicks in. The bridge is bathed in a deep crimson light, and only about one-third of the consoles come spurring to life.

"About fucking time," Atany says with concern as she hits her armrest intercom. "All hands, this is the captain. We have one more Rillian ship out there. Maintain your posts. If you are not on duty, report to damage control or medical triage. Let's get these dicks and move on. Out."

"Fental, where do we stand?"

"Shield down to fifteen percent," she starts, "warp offline, impulse offline, aft torpedo tubes offline, and forward phasers are gone."

"Any good news?"

"We're not dead yet."

"Let's keep it that way. Korah, shut down shields." Everyone sits stunned. "Lock torpedoes and phasers on target."

"What are you up to?" Fental asks, for everyone.

"Fluctuate remaining power throughout the ship."

"I see," Fental says as she complies. "You're going to lure them in closer. Let them think we're dead in space then take them out."

"Helm, as they approach, keep our drift just enough to keep them directly in front of us but don't make it look obvious. On my order, put all power to the thrusters and spin us around like a compass needle one hundred and eighty degrees."

"Aye, Captain," he replies as he sets the controls.

"Tactical, on my command, fire torpedoes, and after, we spin around fire phasers." The lightbulbs go on over everyone's heads.

"We'll keep spinning until we blast their stupid bug asses into whatever they call hell." Everyone on the bridge acknowledges.

The Rillian ship is now on the screen. It approaches slowly as the alliance starship hangs motionless in space. The attack cruiser slowly approaches, cautiously observing the vessel that just took out two others. The bridge crew is anxious, wanting to get this over with. Time seems to have slowed, the ship on the screen appearing not to move.

"We are being scanned," Fental tells her captain.

"Let it go," she orders. "Let them think we're dead."

Thirty seconds go by and the ship is just sitting there.

"What are they up to?" communications officer Reuben asks out loud. It would only take two seconds for his question to be answered.

"Intruder alert. Intruder alert," the cold mechanical voice of the computer answers, seemingly mocking the lieutenant.

"Well," he says, "I guess we know."

"Helm, tactical," the captain shouts, "do it, now!"

"Aye, Captain" is heard in stereo. The weapons fire, and as the ship spins, everyone on the bridge, and the whole ship for that matter, feel the disorientation from the inertial dampeners being damaged. The captain hits her armrest intercom as she straightens in her chair.

"All hands, this is the captain. We've been boarded. We have no room for prisoners. Do what must be done. Out." She activates another control on the armrest.

"Transporter room?" she asks her armrest.

"Transporter room, here," a young lieutenant's nervous voice replies.

"Good, good," Atany says slightly more calm. "Lock on to the Rillians on my ship and beam them off."

"I can't get a transporter lock on their ship because we keep moving," the officer asks with the voice of inexperience.

"Why try? Their ship will be gone in seconds," Atany answers.

"Then where do I beam them?"

"Use your imagination, beam them into space."

"They'll die," the voice answers in near disbelief.

"It's them or you," she tells him.

"I'll begin with the ones closest to the bridge," he answers.

"We all would appreciate that." She deactivates the intercom.

"Are they dead yet?" she yells loudly.

"It's not as easy as you may think," Korah responds.

"Their shields are down, and their weapons are offline. We can disengage anytime."

"I don't think so," she says to Fental. "Finish them," she says to no one in particular.

"Yes, ma'am," comes from the two officers, and after several more revolutions, the Rillian ship starts to withdraw.

"How many of those bugs are still on my ship?"

"Last ones being beamed off now," the transporter operator's voice booms in the room.

"Korah, take them out."

The phasers fire, and after a few seconds, the Rillian attack cruiser explodes in a huge fireball.

"Anything else around us?"

"Negative, Captain," Fental answers.

"Well," Atany says, more relaxed as she sits back in her seat, "that really sucked." Everyone on the bridge agrees.

"Reuben," she continues, "get me a damage report." She turns to her science officer. "Fental, keep a sharp eye around us."

"Will do," she replies coldly. The captain spins back to face front.

"Merah, get us to the Rhinehart Nebula, best possible speed."

"Right away," he responds as he keys in commands. The ship starts to move. The shaking and vibrating have everyone nervously looking around, each silently praying that the ship holds together.

"Controls are sluggish," he reports as he continues to key in commands. "I'm going to keep it at half impulse until engineering okays an increase." He turns his head to face her.

"Very good," she says. "What's our ETA?"

"Eighteen point five days at present speed."

"Understood," she answers.

"Captain," Reuben interrupts, "damage control reports hull breaches on decks three and four, forcefields are holding, warp engines offline but impulse engines are online, all weapons systems offline, environmental control systems are currently under repair, forward power conduits are fused, structural integrity systems are under repair, and about half the secondary systems are under repair."

"Inform them that I want updates every fifteen minutes."

"Aye, Captain," he answers as he does what is ordered.

Three days later finds very few things changed. The hull breaches were the first things to be repaired. Now that there are no holes in the bulkheads, the forcefields have been dropped and the extra power has been diverted to the impulse drive. Speed has been set at three quarter impulse for the last twenty-two hours.

"Two of the forward torpedo tubes are operational, and phaser banks are at half power, Captain," communications officer Roeton reports as Atany takes her seat. "Shields are still inoperative, and aft weapons arrays are still down."

"Any good news?" the captain asks as she sips the coffee she brought onto the bridge with her.

"I'm afraid not, but environmental systems should be back online within the hour, that's as close as it comes," he answers.

"Fental," Atany says as she swings her chair to face her science officer. "Do you have any good news for me?"

"Good is relative, Captain," she answers. "Short-range sensors are still offline, but I'll have long-range sensors up in a few minutes."

"Good, keep it up," she replies as she hits a button on her armrest. "Engineering, when can I have warp drive?" A sense of urgency in her voice.

"Benjamin here, Captain, you'll have warp drive in about four hours, providing I don't get any rough rides."

"We'll do our best up here," she reassures him.

Dinema spins her seat to look at the viewscreen. She stares silently into the darkness on the viewer. The silence is short-lived.

"Long-range sensors are back online but are at seventy-five percent power," Fental says. "Scanning the area." Then after several seconds, she continues, "All clear, so far."

"Keep scanning while you're tweaking the systems," she orders politely.

"Will do, Captain," Fental responds. Fifteen minutes pass.

"Captain," Fental says with some excitement in her voice. "I have two targets on my screen."

"Identification?" she asks.

"Unknown," she replies. "I don't even know if they're really there."

"Explain."

"I just got the sensors back online. It could be a ghost image."

"Could be, but at this point, I'm not going to risk it." She turns to her communications officer. "Roeton, get me hanger deck control."

"Yes, Captain." And after a few seconds, "Hanger deck here," a voice blares from the speakers.

"Ensign Galal, have the ex vees been prepped and readied for launch?"

The bridge crew looks puzzled.

"Yes, ma'am" is the answer.

"Good. Get the pilots from their quarters and have them in the launch bays in five. I'm coming down." She motions to Roeton to terminate the communication, and he does. Atany looks around to see the curious looks being shot to her.

"While we were at Jehovah's service, star command had the rear cargo bays converted to launch tubes for the ex vee fighters."

"What are ex vee fighters?" Fental asks with confusion and anger. "And why didn't you tell us?"

"Ex vee fighters are experimental vee-wing single-seat fighters. They were developed in secret as close-quarter defense. I wanted to wait until a crisis situation and their need imminent and unavoidable before I informed anyone. Star Command wanted secrecy until the last possible moment. As this mission is of such importance and our ship is in the condition that it is in, I think it's time."

The bridge crew agrees, and all return to their duties with a reinvigorated enthusiasm. Atany leaves the bridge with Fental on her heels.

The doors to the turbolift open, and the two women find themselves in the converted cargo area. Coming off the turbolift, they stand about thirty feet from four equally spaced square hatches measuring eight feet by eight feet.

In front of each door there is an ex vee fighter. Each ship is seated on a block that's attached to a grooved track going under the hatch. Fental's walk slows as she studies the ships.

Each ship is fifteen feet long. The body is slightly oval, looking from back to front, measuring about three and a half feet across. There is a round, two-foot-wide-by-seven-foot-long turbo thruster on each side of the hull, extending past the back of the ship about two inches.

Above each turbo is a wing angled up thirty degrees, giving the craft its distinctive "vee" look. On the hull, in front of the engines, is the cockpit. The four feet in front of the cockpit holds the onboard instrument packs—radar, shields, sensors, etc.

Each ship has two phased energy weapons, one on each side of the body, just forward of the cockpit, housed inside a triangle housing that runs down the length of the body, right to the engines.

The flat gray color, mixed with the shiny chrome of the engine intakes and copper and gold conduits, along with the sleek look, makes Fental's heart skip a beat.

If I could fall in love with an inanimate object, this would be it, she thinks to herself. Atany sees the look in her eyes.

"It was love at first sight for me too," she tells Fental with a smile.

The captain and first officer turn to the right and go behind the turbolift where three men and two women are sitting at a table. When the two women come into view, the five stand.

"Welcome, Captain," Ensign Galal, the man in the center, says.

"Captain," the ensign begins. "This is Lieutenant Commander Rigel, in Ex Vee One." He motions to the woman at his right. "And Lieutenant Jullian, in Ex Vee Two." He motions to the man to her right.

"This is Lieutenant Borkin, in Ex Vee Three." He motions to the man at his left. "And finally, Lieutenant Jasmine, in Ex Vee Four," he says, motioning to the woman to his left.

"Sorry we could've met sooner and under better circumstances, but now it's time to earn your pays and put your prototypes to the test."

"What's up, Captain?" Rigel asks.

"You all know we've been through some heavy combat. We are still heavily damaged in key systems, and an unknown vessel came into range of the long-range sensors. The target may only be a sensor ghost, but we need you to go and make sure. If it is a vessel, you are to discover their intent and take appropriate action. As it stands, you four pilots and planes are our only last line of defense. Get out there and take care of business."

All five stand and start toward the fighters with the captain and first officer. The four climb into their cockpits and seal their canopies.

From inside the ships, the pilots open their corresponding doors. Another switch causes the blocks to slide forward until the ship is fully behind the hatch. The heavy hatch doors close with a resounding thud.

Atany and Fental step onto the bridge and take their posts.

"Ex Vee One ready," comes over the communication speakers. "Ex Vee Two ready," Followed by "Ex Vee Three ready." And finally, "Ex Vee Four ready."

"Launch," Atany orders. The pilots press buttons in their ships, and simultaneously, the outer doors of the launch tubes open. And as the air rushes into space, the blocks under the ships thrust forward on a cushion of magnetic energy that acts as a catapult as the pilots activate the engines on their ships.

The combination of the three actions sends the fighters into space at speed in excess of fifteen thousand kilometers an hour. The four fighters break off in different directions, circle around the *Heaven*, and form up two by two.

"Take up a heading of three, two, three, mark seven. Target is at three thousand two hundred kilometers," Lieutenant Levi informs the four pilots.

"Copy that, base," Rigel's voice echoes on the bridge.

"Taking up a heading of three, two, three mark seven. Time to intercept twenty-two minutes."

"Affirmative," Levi says. "Report when you make visual contact."

"Copy that," the pilot says.

The four ships streak through space, heading for their destiny.

On the bridge it is business as usual. Fental is still working on the sensor arrays as damage control teams are all over the ship and the engineering crews try to get the warp drive online.

Ten minutes after the last communications with the fighters, Fental lifts her head from her monitor.

"Captain, sensors are fully operational. Scanning for target," she tells her captain. After a few moments, she continues with her report.

"Target acquisition positive, Captain. It's the Rillians."

"Roeton, inform the fighters about the Rillians," Atany orders.

"Aye, Captain," he says as he complies.

"Copy that, base," the familiar female voice replies. "We will leave channels open so we can coordinate attack strategies."

"Roger that," Levi answers.

"Nine minutes to intercept," the pilot says with confidence in her voice. "Break formation," she orders. "Ex Vee Two, you're with me. Three and Four, heading zero, three, five mark zero, zero, two."

"Roger," Borkin and Jasmine confirm.

Ex Vees One and Two break formation to the left at a slightly negative zee axis. Ex Vees Three and Four break to the right at a slightly positive zee axis and race away. Four minutes go by and the radios remain silent.

"Captain," Fental breaks the silence. "I'm getting strange readings from the Rillian ship."

"Define *strange*."

"It's like the ship is expanding and contracting."

"How's that?" Atany asks with a bizarre confusion.

"At one moment I'm reading normal mass from the ship, then the next reading shows a fifty-percent increase in mass, then several scans later, it's normal again."

"Could it be a glitch in the system?"

"No," Fental says flatly. "I just ran a diagnostic. It's patched together, but everything's working properly."

"We read you, base," comes from Rigel. "We'll keep a sharp eye out."

"Keep trying to figure out those readings, Fental," Atany says.

"Will do, Captain," she replies. Once again the bridge goes quiet.

Five more minutes go by. The bridge crew is getting antsy in anticipation of Rillian contact. Again the silence is broken.

"This is Ex Vee Three. I have a visual on the Rillian ship. She isn't turning to face me, and readings show below-normal power output. I don't think they see us."

"Their sensors may still be down, Captain," Fental volunteers.

"This is Ex Vee One, I'm coming up on the Rillian ship. Power up your phase canons and let's take this bitch down. Ex Vee Two, take up a heading of—holy shit!" Rigel screams.

"What is it?" Atany yells excitedly.

"Behind the Rillian ship!" she shouts. "It's a Chandrakan battle cruiser! Scans show a power buildup. They're charging weapons."

"What about the Rillians?" Atany asks Fental.

"Still nothing," she reports. "Their communications might still be down, so the Chandrakan can't warn them."

"Concentrate attack on the Chandrakan ship," Atany commands.

"Roger that," Rigel responds. "Ex Vee Two, you and I will come up from the belly. Three and Four, you guys strafe from above."

All acknowledge.

Ex Vees One and Two fly in under the Rillian ship, and as they emerge from the aft, they fire their phase canons in unison. Seconds later, Ex Vees Three and Four fire their phase canons down the spine of the ship, explosions occurring at the end of the passes, when the Chandrakan ship loses its shields. The two groups of ships perform a half circle and rollover. As Ex Vees Three and Four cut down the center of the ship from underside, Ex Vees One and Two barrage the spine where the other two had attacked.

As explosions ride down the spine of the ship, four phased energy bolts hit the bridge within a single heartbeat. The first bolt weakens the hull of the bridge. The second bolt blows a hole in the ceiling of the bridge, and before the forcefields could activate, the two remaining bolts vaporize the bridge from the inside. The explosion rips down through the decks below, taking out the computer's central processor units as well as the EPS conduits running under the decks below.

The ship, adrift in space, is without power from the bridge forward to the navigational deflector, with sporadic explosions ripping through its shell.

The four ships converge several kilometers aft of the crippled battle cruiser. As they approach from behind, the fighters break off into two groups, leaving a gap of about two hundred meters between them with the Chandrakan ship in the middle.

Speeding closer, the ships on each side separate vertically, creating now a huge square. The Rillian ship still shows no sign of acknowledging the fighters. The fighters are now four kilometers away and closing fast, with only seconds to take action.

Rigel gives an order. "On my mark, start strafing. Go for the nacelles, weapons arrays, and the bridge."

All three pilots acknowledge the order. All is quiet. Seconds tick by slowly. Now it begins.

"Fire!" Rigel yells. "Blast the fuckers!"

Atany smiles at Fental, who smiles back, upon hearing how this pilot speaks.

The four fighters start firing nearly simultaneously, hitting both nacelles, and rock the ship not only left and right but up and down as well, sending crewmen to the floors with force. A slight turn sends the two ships firing from above the battle cruiser straight at the bridge.

With the cruiser's forcefields working at minimum power, and the precision flying and firing skills of the pilots, a series of energy bolts enter the already vaporized bridge, and after a short series of violent explosions, the front quarter of the hull blows away from the rest of the ship. The fighters veer off and rendezvous at a safe distance.

Explosions within the nacelles increase as the main hull vents atmosphere and crewmen into space. Within seconds, explosions rip through the hull to the engine room.

The first blast in the engine room takes out the EPS conduit feeding the control system computers. Darkness envelops the room except for the light in the reaction control chamber, the light caused by several billions of terawatts of energy being created by the mixing of matter and antimatter.

The second blast shatters the reaction control chamber, and as matter and antimatter start venting into the room, there is no time for a third energy bolt to impact. Antimatter hits a stream of air, and the remnant of the ship disintegrates in a brilliant ball of intense light.

The shockwave from the explosion pushes the front part of the hull, earlier separated from the rest of the vessel, toward the damaged Rillian ship at a greatly increased speed.

"Holy shit!" Lieutenant Jasmine says. "Did you see that?"

"What's going on out there?" Atany demands.

"All I see are blue spots," Lieutenant Jullian says.

"Me too," replies Borkin.

"That was great," Jasmine answers, with excitement heavy in her voice. Without warning, the screams of all four pilots fill the bridge.

"What the fuck is going on out there?!" Atany screams.

The screaming stops suddenly. Rigel speaks again. "Guys, look at that."

"Holy fuck," one replies.

"Fucking ay," another says, followed by a cheer from the third.

As the light from the matter-antimatter explosion fades, the four pilots can see the Rillian ship. Two kilometers aft of the ship, off its port bow, they see the forward section of the Chandrakan cruiser speeding toward the vessel.

The out-of-control section slams into the Rillian ship, ripping off the port nacelle and upper deck assembly. The ship lists and starts to spin like a saucer, plasma spewing from the connecting corridor where the nacelle used to be. A dim blue haze covers the massive opening on the top of the ship, where the upper deck assembly was connected, showing that the force fields are in place.

"Sorry, Captain," Rigel's disembodied voice fills the bridge again. "Lots going on. The Chandrakan battle cruiser has been completely destroyed. The Rillian ship is severely damaged, and if you give us a few more minutes, we'll blow their asses away."

"What was all that screaming?" the captain asks with concern.

"We were hit by the shockwave from the explosion of the cruiser, but everything checks out and we're ready to finish this."

"Then by all means, dispatch those dickheads to the hell they deserve," Atany tells the fighter pilots.

"We're on it, Captain. Be back shortly."

"Confirmed."

The four fighters form up in a wedge formation and speed toward the crippled, spinning ship.

"Careful of that plasma stream," Lieutenant Jasmine reminds the others.

The other three pilots acknowledge.

As they streak closer, they pull up in a positive zee axis climb. About three kilometers later, they roll into a one hundred and eighty -degree turn and speed toward the Rillian craft from above.

The four ships form into a tight box formation, bottom to bottom, as they approach the enemy ship. At twenty-five hundred meters' distance, they start firing. All the phased energy bolts are concentrated on the forcefields protecting the interior of the vessel.

Within a few seconds, the forcefields fall, and dozens of energy bolts slam into the bulkheads of the ship, causing mass explosions on each deck as bolt after bolt strike, then break through to the next deck, continuing until they finish blasting through to the bottom bulkhead.

The Rillian ship explodes in a ball of light as brilliant as the Chandrakan ship several minutes earlier. The four Ex Vee fighters streak across the void of space, en route to their rendezvous with the *Heaven*.

Chapter 5

Captain's log, stardate 30075.42. The Ex Vees proved themselves indispensable during our recent incident with the Rillian and Chandraka. The fighters have been taken back aboard. Repairs are nearing completion, and we are en route to the Reinhart nebula, ETA at current speed is thirteen point five days.

"Captain," Lieutenant Roeton interrupts, "I have Commander Benjamin in engineering on the horn."

"Patch him through to my chair."

After a second, a voice booms from her armrest. "Captain, I'm ready to test the warp drive. Increase speed slowly."

"Okay," she answers, leaving the communications channel open. "Levi, bring us to warp one."

"Yes, ma'am," he says as he manipulates the controls. The static star pattern on the screen changes in an instant to the streaking stars that indicate faster-than-light travel. A few seconds pass.

"Benjamin, how are my engines holding together?" Atany asks.

"All systems showing normal," he answers.

"Very good then," she stares at the screen. "Warp three," she orders.

Levi manipulates the controls once again. The digital indicator on his control panel steadily increases and, in a matter of seconds, goes from one point zero, zero to three point zero, zero.

"Warp three, Captain," he informs her.

"Engineering?" Atany asks aloud.

"All systems are still in the green, but I can't guarantee how long they'll hold," Benjamin replies. "But I wouldn't suggest you push it."

"Agreed," she says. "We'll maintain warp three, and you fix my engines. Let me know when we can go faster."

"Deal," he says, and the line goes quiet.

"Levi," Atany continues, "what's our ETA now?"

"ETA now nine point two hours."

"Much better," Atany comments as she sits back in her seat.

Hawking sits back in his seat, away from his monitor. He tips his head back while rubbing his eyes. He lets out a deep exhale in an attempt to relax. He stands and, after a few seconds, makes his way to the replicator.

"Give me a glass of water, please," he says to the machine.

"Specify temperature," the computer responds.

"I don't care," he states, "as long as it's cold." A second passes.

"Specify temperature," the computer repeats coldly.

"What the fuck?" Hawking asks rhetorically.

"Please specify the parameters of the request," the computer replies.

"Thirty-six degrees Fahrenheit," he answers with anger heavy in his voice. After a few seconds, he realizes how ridiculous it is to be angry at a machine. He starts laughing.

A second after Hawking answers, the recessed shelf within the unit glows with a brilliant light, and the replicator hums. Within two seconds, a spiraling tornado of flickering lights appears in the center of the recessed shelf.

During the next two seconds, the flickering lights glow brighter and brighter until a glowing cylinder of light appears, all along the pitch of the machine's hum gets higher.

In an instant, the pitch of the hum gets lower and slower. As the sound fades, the light also fades, and on the shelf is a tall glass of cold water. He picks it up and walks back to his seat. He takes a long, slow drink. He puts his glass down and stretches. He exhales long and slow.

Hawking focuses his attention to the padds on the desk, the padds that show the glyphs on the artifact boxes.

"I've gotta figure this shit out," he says out loud to himself. He goes back to staring intensely at the padds, occasionally sipping his water.

Thirty minutes go by, and Atany continues to stare at the main viewscreen. The rest of the bridge crew are monitoring their systems.

"Captain," Roeton speaks. "Damage control reports all weapon systems, fore and aft, have been repaired and are fully energized. Shields will be at full power within the hour."

"That's good news," she says out loud.

"Captain," Roeton speaks again. "Professor Hawking is on the line."

"Put him down here," she replies, pointing at her armrest.

"Go ahead," Roeton informs her, and she hits the control.

"What is it, Professor?" she asks.

"Captain," Hawking says with a noticeable excitement. "I need to speak with Shawn. Can I have an open channel?" he asks.

"Sure. Is everything all right?"

"I think so, but I really must confer with Shawn first. I will let you know if what I'm thinking pans out."

"I'll have Roeton set it up, and he'll let you know when contact has been established," she answers.

"Excellent. Thank you, Captain."

"My pleasure, Professor." A smile slides across her face as she replies.

"Roeton, get Brantax control to establish a link with the Maroonna archeological dig site then let Aristotle know."

"On it, Captain."

Five minutes pass by without incident. The whooshing of the turbolift door causes everyone to look in that direction. The captain spins to see Lieutenant Commander Benjamin, the chief engineer, step onto the bridge. He turns left and sits at the first console, the engineering control console. He activates the station's computer interface.

"Captain," Benjamin starts. "I've got the engines as repaired as I can without a starbase layover. People are in position. Increase speed at your discretion. I'll monitor everything from here."

"Very good," she says as she turns to her science officer. "It's about time we get some good news, ay, Fental?"

"Absofuckinlutely," Dutona answers with a smile and chuckle.

Atany spins to face the viewscreen. "Levi, increase to warp six . . . slowly," she orders.

"Aye, Captain," he responds and manipulates the controls once again.

The indicator slowly increases. In fifteen seconds, the reading goes from three point zero, zero up to six point zero, zero.

"Warp six," Levi announces just as a deep beeping sound comes from the engineering console. Benjamin looks at the power flow chart schematics and starts keying in commands. The beeping stops.

"Report!" Atany shouts.

"Intermix formula was a little rich. It's been adjusted, and all readings are normal," Benjamin informs her and the rest of the bridge crew.

"Helm, stay at warp six and give me an ETA."

"ETA is thirty-eight minutes," he replies.

"My engines will hold together," Benjamin comfortingly tells the captain and crew.

Fifteen minutes into the journey, Roeton informs the captain, "Professor Hawking would like to speak to you, Captain."

"Down here again, Roeton," she answers, and in a second, Roeton says, "Ready, Captain."

She acknowledges and hits the armrest control. "Yes, Professor, what can I do for you?" she asks.

"That we can talk about later," he starts, "but right now I need you and Dutona to come down here."

"What's up, Professor?" she asks.

"I have news, but I need the two of you to assist for a short time."

"Can it wait a bit, Professor?"

"It's about the glyphs on the artifact boxes, Captain."

The two women perk up a bit.

"On that note, Professor, we will be arriving at the Rhinehart Nebula in just over twenty minutes, then we start the search." She takes a breath and continues, "We will be down momentarily."

"Thank you, Captain."

She deactivates the communications console and stands. Fental stands, and the two women head to and step into the turbolift.

The doors to the cargo bay / laboratory open, and the women enter to find Hawking staring at the four padds on the desk while inputting data on another padd.

"What's going on, Professor?" Atany asks as the two approach the desk.

He looks up, surprised. "Ah, Captain, Lieutenant," he says with a huge smile. "Shawn and I have deciphered nearly all the glyphs."

The two women smile widely.

"The glyphs are descriptions of the six components and instructions on assembling and integrating them."

"For what purpose?" Fental asks.

"Opening a portal of some kind to get to the Forzak homeworld."

"Then what's wrong? You seem to have it under control," Atany says.

"I can translate and record, but I don't know shit about all this technical stuff. That's where you two beautiful women come into play. You know all that stuff," he explains.

"All right, Professor, we can do that," Atany says and continues, "Do you have the location of the last artifact yet?"

"No. I only have part of the clue," he says.

"The rest of the clue is on the artifact that we're picking up now."

"Exactly," Hawking confirms.

"We'll be arriving at the Rhinehart Nebula in about ten minutes," the captain starts. "Once there, we still have to find the artifact. You work on those instructions until we find the artifact then get us the location of the last one, and while we're heading there, you can translate the newest one. What do you say?"

"I can work with that, Captain," he answers.

"Good. Fental and I will return to the bridge, and we'll be down again after we find artifact number five." The two women head to the door. Midway to the door, Atany stops and turns to face Hawking. "One more thing, Professor," Dinema says.

"What's that, Captain?"

"What you said on the intercom before we came down here?" she says somewhat questioningly.

He nods in acknowledgement.

"I'll be down later to continue that discussion," she says with the sly, seductive smile that makes his heart skip a beat.

"I'm looking forward to it." He smiles back.

"So am I," she says as she turns and walks out of the room.

"Captain," Levi says, "we will reach the leading edge of the nebula in two minutes."

"Very good," Atany says. She looks over at Fental. "Dutona, start scanning for the artifact's signal. With luck we can find it quickly."

"Yes, Captain," she acknowledges and buries her face in her work.

"Slow to impulse," the captain orders.

"Aye, Captain," comes from Levi, and instantaneously, the streaking star pattern disappears and is replaced by a seemingly static star field with a faint white haze in the center of screen, reaching across the full length of the viewscreen.

"Now that we've dropped out of warp, we will arrive at the nebula in six point four minutes," Levi tells the captain.

"Sacar, do you see anything on your tactical scanners?" Atany asks. "This is when we should be attacked by somebody," she finishes with a cautious giggle.

"Negative, Captain," he reports. "My scanners show nothing."

"Still, I'm not going to take any chances. Go to yellow alert. We'll maintain that posture until we recover the artifact."

"Yes, Captain," he replies as he keys in the appropriate commands.

The yellow alert klaxon sounds throughout the ship three times as the indicator lights on all desks bathe the halls in yellow light.

"Three minutes until nebula barrier," Levi volunteers.

The bridge remains quiet. The hazy field of the nebula fills the screen at a steady pace. About thirty seconds after Levi's announcement, all the surrounding stars are gone.

"Fental?" Atany half asks.

"Still nothing," she answers.

"If you widened the sensor field, would it still be possible to pick up the signal?" Curiosity fills the captain's voice.

"Yes," she replies. "The problem with that is we'll only get a generalized location."

"Like a directional beacon until we get close, then we narrow the beam and pinpoint the location."

"That'll work, I think."

"Let's try it."

"Already on it, Captain." She makes the adjustments to her equipment and starts to analyze the data.

"One minute until nebula penetration," Levi says.

"Anything yet?" Atany asks Fental.

"Nothing, but remember, though, that all that ionized gas will significantly reduce the sensor's efficiency."

"I know, I know. If you can come up with another idea, I'm all ears."

"Not at the moment, no, I can't," Fental responds.

"Okay, then," Atany adds, "stay focused. Let's find this thing and get out of here."

"Amen, Captain," she answers as she buries her face back near the monitor and focuses on the readings.

"Sacar, do tactical sensors show any bodies within the nebula?"

"Not at present, but there have been planets and asteroids charted within the nebula," he answers.

The ship noticeably slows down as the shields make contact with the ionized gases of the nebula. As the vessel enters, the main viewscreen starts to distort as the ionized energy affects the exposed electronic components. The distortion on the screen is intermittent but annoying.

Two hours pass yet yield nothing. The *Heaven* passes several rogue asteroids and two dwarf planets. No signal is detected. The ship moves slowly yet steadily. Each member of the bridge crew is showing eye strain due to staring at the viewscreen or their monitors.

"Captain," Sacar says nonchalantly. "Another series of rogue asteroids at zero, two, two mark zero, one, zero. Distance fifteen thousand kilometers."

"Lay in a course, Levi," Atany orders. The vessel lazily changes course and heads toward the asteroids. A few seconds pass.

"Captain, I'm picking up a signal. Very faint, but it is the artifact."

"Where is it?"

"All I can say, for certain, is that the signal is in the general direction of the asteroids we are approaching."

"That's good enough for me," Atany says as she turns her attention to the helmsman. "Levi, how long until we reach the asteroids?" the captain inquires.

"Two point five minutes, Captain."

"Right on," Atany replies. "Levi, patch helm control into the science station." She spins to face Fental. "Dutona, narrow the sensor beams and pinpoint the location. You'll have control of the helm."

"Gee, thanks," Fental responds. "No pressure here." She glares back into her monitor and makes the necessary course corrections from the panel to her right.

"Helm, read out the distance in increments of a thousand."

"Aye, Captain," he says. He keys in commands and looks at the indicator. "On my mark it will be thirteen thousand kilometers." Several seconds pass. "And . . . mark, thirteen thousand kilometers."

Ten seconds pass.

"Twelve thousand kilometers."

Ten more seconds pass.

"Eleven thousand kilometers."

This continues for two minutes.

"Captain," Fental interrupts. "My instruments are reading multiple asteroids. I am having difficulty managing both procedures. Levi, take over helm control to maneuver around the asteroids, and I'll send you course corrections."

"Yes, ma'am," he says, "when you're ready."

"Helm is yours, Mr. Levi," Fental tells him.

The ship maneuvers around the small rocks lazily floating in the ionized gases.

"Do you have a pinpoint location for the signal?"

"Still narrowing the focus of the beams. I can tell you we are five hundred kilometers from the signal. Dead ahead."

"Get me the transporter room," Atany tells Kohath. He makes the connection without saying a word.

"Transporter room here." A disembodied voice fills the bridge.

"Can you get a transporter lock on the artifact by isolating its signal and beam it to the cargo bay?"

"With the amount of ionic interference, we need to be within fifty kilometers of the signal."

"Okay then, Levi, Dutona, get us within fifty kilometers. Keep tied into the transporter room. Don't get any closer than absolutely necessary."

The two acknowledge as Atany sits back in her seat, intensely staring at the viewscreen.

For the next ten minutes, the ship slowly makes its way through the electronic discharge of the ionized gases floating in the nebula. It maneuvers around asteroids as shimmering fingers of energy dance over the edge of the ship's shields.

"We are approximately seventy-five kilometers from the signal," Fental says. "Still can't get a pinpoint location. Levi, course correction. Six degrees starboard."

"Six degrees starboard," Levi repeats as he adjusts the ship's course.

"Got it," Dutona says after nearly a minute. "Directly ahead. Sixty kilometers."

"Sacar, what are you picking up on tactical?" the captain asks.

"I have a dwarf planet ahead and at mark zero, zero, three."

"Adjusting course," Levi volunteers. "We'll be in transporter range in about ninety seconds."

Atany hits the button on the armrest. "Transporter room, make every effort to lock onto the signal as soon as possible," she says.

"Will do, Captain." The signal goes quiet. Forty-five seconds pass.

"Transporter room to bridge," comes from the ship's speakers.

"Go ahead," Atany says aloud.

"Transport complete. The artifact is in the cargo bay with Professor Hawking."

"Right on," Atany says then turns to Levi. "Helm, get us out of here."

"Aye, Captain, consider it done," he responds.

The ship makes a gentle half circle and heads in a straight line out of the nebula. The sparkling discharges lessen as the ship approaches the outer edge of the nebula.

The bridge crew stare at the viewscreen, waiting for the interference from the nebula to clear. The blotchy images between the snowy screen interference show the hazy gases outside of the ship. With no warning, the screen clears to its perfect picture as the ship exits the nebula.

"We're out of the nebula," Levi tells the crew. "Course, Captain?"

"Keep us here for now," she answers as she turns to the communications officer. "Roeton, contact engineering and tell them they have an undetermined amount of time to do whatever they can to reinforce the engine repairs. Dutona and I will be with Professor Hawking, trying to determine our next location." She motions to Fental as she gets up, and the two step onto the turbolift.

The two women enter the cargo bay / lab to find Professor Hawking already at work recording the glyphs on a new padd. They approach him unobserved.

"Hello, Professor," Atany says politely.

"Aahh!" he shouts as his body spasms from being startled, the padd flying from his hand. Fental catches it as it soars inches over her head.

"What the fuck! I asked you not to do that."

"I'm sorry, Professor," the captain says, nearly laughing.

"Me too," he replies as he starts to laugh. Fental passes the padd back to Hawking as the three laugh together for several seconds.

Chapter 6

Captain's log, stardate 30080.17. Thanks to the brilliance of Professor Hawking and his associates on Brantax Three, we have determined the location of the final artifact. We are en route to Orancara Four to retrieve it. ETA nine hours. Professor Hawking will continue to translate the glyphs into a readable instruction manual of sorts.

"Long-range sensors are clear, Captain," Fental reports.
"Tactical sensors show nothing following," Sacar adds. "Shields and all weapons systems are holding at one hundred percent."

"That's the best thing I've heard in a while," the captain says. "Roeton, get me engineering."

"Go ahead, Captain," Roeton replies.

"Benjamin, how are my engines doing?"

"I feel a bit more confident about them. I got some of the systems patched up okay, but others are bypassed."

"Confident enough to go to warp eight?"

"Absolutely, and given some time, I cou—"

"You have as much time as the Rillians, Chandrakan, and Horatha give you. The more you get done, the better off we'll be when they decide to attack, so keep at it."

"Don't worry, Captain, we'll be ready," he answers.

"I know you will. Out." She looks at screen. "Levi, warp eight."

"Warp eight, Captain. We are now five point five hours out."

"Good. On that note, I'm going to my quarters. Contact me in four and a half hours. Until then, do not bother me." Atany gets up and gets on the turbolift.

Beep, beep, beep. The chime of the intercom wakes the captain. She stirs under her covers. The chimes ring again, and this time the captain gets up and activates the controls.

"Atany here. Thanks, bridge, I'll be up shortly." She gets up and heads into the sonic shower. When she finishes, she gets dressed and heads out the door.

The turbolift door opens, and Atany steps onto the bridge, coffee in hand, along with a snack from the mess hall. She takes her seat.

"Report," she says then takes a bite of her fruit.

"We'll arrive at Orancara Four in fifteen minutes," Lieutenant Merah, the night duty helmsman, reports.

"No vessels within sensor range," Lieutenant Korah, the night tactical officer, tells her.

"Nothing unusual to report, Captain," responds Lieutenant Aaron from the science station.

The turbolift door opens, and Fental steps onto the bridge. She walks over and stands to the captain's right. An ensign walks up to the captain and hands her reports that need her signature.

She looks over the reports and signs them. She hands the padd back to the ensign, who walks away silently.

"Captain, Professor Hawking would like to speak to you," communications officer Reuben informs Atany.

"Send it here," she replies.

"Can I come to the bridge, Captain? I have some news you should hear now," Aristotle states.

"It's advantageous you called professor. By all means, come to the bridge," she replies as a slight grin forms on her face.

Two minutes later, the turbolift door opens, and Hawking comes onto the bridge. Atany spins to the sound of the door, and when she sees Hawking, a huge smile sweeps uncontrollably across her face. When Hawking sees her smile, he feels a smile of his own.

"Good morning, Captain," he says through his smile. "Ah, Fental, I'm glad you're here as well."

"Hello, Professor, what's up?" she asks.

"While doing the translating, I found the end of the instructions. It makes reference to spatial coordinates, coordinates that we need to be at when we activate the device that we'll be assembling."

"That's quite the coincidence, Professor," Atany tells him. "We'll be arriving at Orancara Four in about ten minutes. You and Fental plot our next course through the science station and feed it to helm control. After we pick up the artifact, we'll head directly there."

"Excellent," Aristotle says as he and Fental walk over to the science station.

Lieutenant Aaron stands to allow Dutona to sit. They start working on inputting the data.

"Five minutes until orbit," Merah informs the captain.

"Drop out of warp when we pass the third moon."

"Aye, Captain" is the response. More reports are brought to the captain to be signed.

About four minutes later, the ship drops out of warp and the streaking stars disappear and the planet Orancara Four is now in the center of the screen. To the left of the planet, but on the far side, is the inner moon, and to the right, about one third of the distance to the planet, is the second moon.

"Captain," Lieutenant Aaron says with confusion, "I'm picking up readings, but they can't be right."

"Explain," she says, "and be precise." Dutona perks up.

"I was preparing to scan for the signal upon orbit, but I'm already picking it up."

"That's not possible," Fental interrupts as she walks toward the science station. "Not this far out."

"That's not all," Aaron continues. "It's coming from behind us."

"What?" She thinks for a second. "Full stop," she orders as she spins to face the science station.

Fental is already at work, reviewing Aaron's findings. It only takes her a few seconds.

"He's right, Captain," Fental reports. "The signal is close by. I need a minute to pinpoint the exact location."

Everyone sits in silence while Fental studies the readings on her screen. The silence lasts two minutes.

"Set course one, six, zero mark three, three, two," she says.

"Course laid in. Full impulse," Lieutenant Merah replies.

The ship turns left a half circle then angles itself to a slight positive zee axis. Directly in front of the ship, in the center of the main viewscreen, is Orancara Four C, the planet's third moon.

"The signal is coming from dead ahead," Fental informs the captain.

"What do we know about that moon?" Atany asks.

"There is nothing, until now, remarkable with this moon," Fental answers. "No magnetic field, no atmosphere, no life, no rotation. Just a big rock orbiting Orancara Four."

"Well then, let's find this artifact," the captain orders.

Orancara Four C may be just a rock, but big does not describe it. It is the size of a dwarf planet, pitted with asteroid impact craters and fissures that are miles deep. The *Heaven* glides into orbit one hundred kilometers above the surface.

"Have you located the artifact yet?" Atany inquires after twenty minutes in orbit.

"Not yet. Though there is no magnetic field, there is something interfering with my scans," Dutona replies. "I have to track the signal like we did in the nebula. Nothing can be easy."

"I hear that," Atany responds. "Let me know when you find something. I'll be right here."

"It won't be long. Continue on this course," Fental says. Minutes tick by slowly, quietly.

A strange beep is heard apart from the normal sounds of the bridge station's computers and draws the attention of all the bridge crew. The sound comes from the science station. Fental responds to the noise.

"Report," Atany commands after a few seconds.

"The artifact has been located."

"Great," Atany replies. "Where is it?" she asks. She gets no answer. "Fental?" Atany asks again.

"There's a discrepancy," Fental reports.

"Discrepancy?" the captain asks. "What discrepancy? You know I don't like discrepancies."

"Give me a moment, Captain. I'll figure this out," Fental assures her.

"That's what I pay you for." They both smile.

"Okay," Fental says after several moments. "The artifact is in a ravine, three point two kilometers deep in the ravine. Readings show there is no ambient atmosphere around the signal."

"In Utorian, please, so I can understand it," the captain jokes.

"It's located in a cavern, which has long since collapsed," she replies.

"So," the captain continues, "it's buried."

"That is what I said at the beginning."

"I know." Atany laughs lightly as she activates a control on her armrest.

"Transporter room, do you have a lock on the artifact?"

"Almost, Captain. I have to boost the signal gain to make up for the density of the area around it," Galal explains. "I need a few more seconds to get it."

"Take your time. We need that artifact in as pristine shape as possible."

"No problem, Captain," Galal says and then silence. A long five seconds go by. "Transport complete. The artifact is with Professor Hawking."

"Right on. Good job," Atany finishes and deactivates the armrest unit.

The captain stands and looks at her first officer. "Fental, give the coordinates Aristotle gave you earlier to helm."

"Yes, Captain," she answers as she complies.

"Lieutenant Merah," Atany continues, "when you get the coordinates, set a course and get us there at warp three." She walks over to the science station.

"Course laid in, and we are on our way," Merah replies. "ETA four point seven, five days."

"Very good" is her response.

"Finished," Fental says just as the captain arrives.

"You're with me," Atany says. "We are going to help Hawking figure out what these artifacts can do."

"Excellent. I'm ready," she replies as she stands. The two women start walking toward the turbolift.

"Reuben." The captain stops at her communications officer. "Contact Lieutenant Commander Benjamin, Ensign Diana, and physicists Ahijah and Bakkiah. Have them meet us in Professor Hawking's lab."

"Yes, Captain," Reuben answers and begins doing as ordered.

The two women enter the turbolift.

"Why are you having Benjamin, Diana, Bakkiah, and Ahijah meet us?" Fental asks.

"Hawking's translation says that these artifacts create a device to open a vortex," Atany answers, and Fental nods in agreement. Atany continues, "I grabbed the chief engineer, and Diana can use the experience. I'm leaving engineering in the hands of some with some experience."

"Very logical," Fental commends. "But why Bakkiah and Ahijah?"

"If we're going to open some kind of vortex, I need to know exactly what kind of vortex. You'll be busy doing other things. So they'll do the leg work, and you'll look over their findings before we begin."

"Oh? What will I be doing?"

"You'll be helping Hawking and me put this thing together."

"Works for me," Fental responds.

The two women now find themselves standing in front of the cargo bay door being used as a lab. Within seconds, they are joined by the others that were called by the captain.

"What's up, Captain?" Benjamin asks.

"I'll explain inside," she answers as she rings the doorbell. The door slides open, and Professor Hawking is standing in the entryway.

"A party?" Hawking says with a smile aimed at the captain. "If you would have called first, I would have cleaned up a bit," he jokes as he steps back inside, allowing the six crewmen in. The door closes after the six enter the room.

"What's going on, Captain?" Hawking asks as they walk toward the row of boxes of various sizes, on their tables, across the room.

"First things first, Professor," Atany starts. "Introductions as well as explanations are forthcoming."

Atany walks up to the artifacts and turns to face the six people, now in a half circle, behind her.

"For those of you who don't know, this is Professor Aristotle Hawking"—she points to the professor, who is standing to her immediate left—"the foremost authority on the Forzak Empire." She raises her hand and starts from the right.

"Professor, you know Fental. Next to her are Ensigns Ahijah and Bakkiah, my physicists. They are going to determine the nature of the vortex. Next to them are Lieutenant Commander Benjamin, my chief engineer, and Ensign Diana, by you, is my engineer's mate. They're here to help us figure out how to put all this shit together."

"Excellent, Captain, but you are about five minutes premature. I have to record images of the glyphs on the sixth artifact. After that, we can figure out how to open them."

"By all means, Professor," the captain says apologetically.

"Thanks," he says as he grabs an unused padd from the desk and begins to record the glyphs. It takes him just under five minutes to finish. He walks over to the desk and places the padd by the others and joins the others, who are examining the artifact at the left end of the row.

Hawking grabs the padd with the information collected about that specific artifact. He walks over to the others, who are inspecting the box, holding the mysterious artifact.

"According to my translation, there is a catch on the box that will release the five sides. The catch is a symbol within a glyph."

"All right," Atany says. "Benjamin and Ahijah, you two work on the first one. Diana and Bakkiah, you two are on the next one. Fental and I will work on the big one. Professor, translate that last box and table."

Everyone acknowledges the captain's orders, and they break up in their appropriate teams and start examining their respective artifacts.

"Please be careful, everyone. These artifacts are very old. We don't know what condition the components inside are in."

Again everyone acknowledges the information.

Each member of each team begins to gently push on each of the symbols within each of the glyph on the boxes. Thirty minutes go by and none of the boxes have yet to be opened. Annoyance starts to show on their faces.

"Hey!" Diana shouts with excitement. "I found one." She presses the symbol, and it depresses. Everyone stops and looks at her. Each time she presses the symbol, a light click can be heard. Nothing happens. She tries it several more times, and with each press, the same click is heard, and again, nothing happens.

"Professor," Atany says with confusion as she looks toward the desk. She sees Hawking approaching Diana and follows him with her eyes, saying nothing else. Diana looks up at Hawking, confused.

"I saw," he responds, equally confused. "Give me a second. I'll figure this out." He looks closely at the symbols within the glyph, as do the others. Ahijah notices a symbol within a symbol. It takes a number of seconds before her mind comprehends the meaning of what she is looking at. Her eyes suddenly pop open, and a smile appears on her face.

"I got it!" she shouts in near disbelief. "I got it. Everyone, grab a corner. I don't know what's going to happen when I activate this."

Everyone gathers around and holds on to the corners. Hawking walks over to Ahijah.

"What did you find?" he asks.

She looks shyly back at him. "See this symbol?" She points to a square with four short vertical lines protruding from the bottom.

He nods silently in agreement.

"It's in the glyph here and here." She points to the two glyphs directly below each other.

He looks at her, unimpressed.

"Look in the lower right corner of each symbol," she says with a bit more confidence, since she found something that the expert missed.

His eyes grow wide when he sees what she hinted at. Atany looks over.

"See the small single line in the corner?" she asks her captain.

"Yes, I do," she says as Ahijah presses it in. It clicks. She runs her finger down to the next one. She skips over it and goes down one more.

"This symbol has two lines in the corner," she states as she presses the symbol. It depresses and clicks. She moves her finger to the glyph she just passed over.

"This one has three lines," she states again as she presses the symbol. A click is heard.

Within half a second of the third click, a series of new clicks can be heard along the bottom four edges of the box. Within seconds, the clicks stop. Fental and Benjamin grab the box and lift. They are both taken by surprise at how light the material is. They lift the box off like a five-sided cover. They put it on the floor and turn to stare in amazement at an object not seen in over a thousand years.

The object hidden for a millennium looks very unremarkable. It is a rectangle box two meters wide by two meters high by two and a half meters long. On the top of the box is a raised panel, angled upward for easy viewing from what appears to be the back side. On the raised panel is a row of fifteen small square lights. Under the lights are two toggle switches and a slide control.

On the "front" of this unit, there are two prongs sticking out from near the center. Each prong is ten centimeters in diameter and protrudes fifteen centimeters. The "back" of the unit is identical to the "front."

Ensign Bakkiah takes out a tricorder and scans the artifact. After studying the results, he scans the unit again. He looks confused.

"What is it, ensign?" Atany asks.

"These readings," he answers.

"What readings?" she continues.

"Exactly," he says.

"What the fuck are you saying?" Anger now in her voice.

"What I'm saying is . . . there are no readings. It's impossible, but there are no readings," he says back with slight defiance.

Fental takes the tricorder and runs a scan. "Everything gives off some kind of readings," Fental reminds Bakkiah as she runs the scan. Her face displays the same look of confusion that still remains on Bakkiah's face.

"I am aware of that, Lieutenant. That's why I ran the second scan, like you," he says as his face gets flush with anger.

"I'm sorry, ensign," she retorts. "I know you know how to do this or you wouldn't be here." The second scan finishes.

"He's right, Captain. There are no readings at all."

"What do you make of it?" she asks both.

"There is nothing that can explain this," Bakkiah tells her.

"I concur," Fental replies. The room is silent for a moment.

"That's a mystery for another time," Atany says definitively. "Right now we have to get this device installed and active." She looks over at Hawking. "Professor, do you know what component this is?"

"If I'm not mistaken, this is the universal plasma phase converter. This unit will phase our plasma energy to the frequency capable of powering the rest of the equipment."

"Now that we have an idea of what to look for, let's get back to it," Atany orders. The groups return to searching their boxes. Five minutes go by and the series of clicks can be heard, followed by "Hell yeah!" from Diana.

Diana and Bakkiah lift the top off and put it over by the first. The component on the table is three quarters of a meter by three quarters of a meter square by fifty centimeters deep. The face is covered by inlaid controls, contrary to the tactile style of the controls on the first unit.

The "front" of this unit has prongs similar to the ones on the other component, just a bit longer and slightly wider. There is nothing else on this component.

Atany looks at Hawking. "What's this, Professor?" she inquires.

"This is the system operation control unit. This unit will connect to the plasma phase converter after it's installed. This controls the device once it's powered up," Hawking explains.

Fental finds the locking code for the artifact she and Atany were working on. Not only does the clicking run along the bottom, it also runs up one side, across the top and down the other side. Being one of the two largest artifacts, its cover comes off in two pieces. The two halves are removed. The component is the shape of a huge half circle.

"This component is the deflector frequency modulation controller. It mounts to the exterior of the deflector dish and adjusts the deflector frequency to create the vortex that we must travel through," Hawking tells them. "The other large artifact contains a second controller."

"Speaking of that, Professor, will you give Ensigns Ahijah and Bakkiah everything you've uncovered about the power specs?"

"For what purpose?" he asks.

"They are going to try to determine exactly what kind of energies we will be attempting to create and, ultimately, the properties of the vortex we are trying to open," she answers.

While Hawking gets the data for the two physicists, Atany, Fental, Benjamin, and Diana move to the next two artifacts. It takes only a matter of minutes before the fourth artifact opens, followed quickly by the fifth.

Hawking identifies the fourth component as the plasma intermix amplifier chamber. This component exponentially amplifies the power of the plasma and prepares it for the next component. As he explains this to Atany and Fental, Benjamin and Diana unlock the sixth cover.

While the two engineers move the two covers, Hawking tells them about the next component. It is the pre-fire cooling chamber. This unit supercools the plasma before it hits the deflector frequency modulator controllers.

The component in the last box is the same large half-circle deflector frequency modulator controller.

"Ahijah, Bakkiah." Atany looks at the two from across the desk where the seven are standing now that the six components have been unboxed and identified. "I want the two of you to return to your lab and continue working. Identify any potential hazards we may encounter, on top of the other things y'all have to do."

The two acknowledge and return to their lab.

"It's up to the five of us to figure out how all this is supposed to go together," Atany tells the rest.

"We should move the components to engineering. That's where the bulk of these components will be installed," Benjamin suggests.

"Very good," Atany agrees. "Benjamin and Diana, get with the transporter room and get these components there. Fental, check in with the bridge. We'll meet in engineering in fifteen minutes."

All agree and comply, leaving Atany and Hawking alone.

As soon as the door closes, Atany turns to Hawking, who is already standing inches behind her. A huge smile sweeps across her face and, when he sees her beautiful smile, finds a smile uncontrollably glued to his face.

Now standing face-to-face, Hawking wraps his arm around Atany's waist and pulls her in close. He plants his lips hard against hers, their tongues darting in and out of each other's mouths. As his tongue massages hers, a low moan of pleasure rises from deep inside Dinema.

The air around Hawking fills with the intoxicating aroma that sends his mind spinning out of control. A moan stirs within him. When Atany hears Aristotle's low moan, she pulls him in closer, kissing him harder. His knees start to buckle.

Hawking sits down heavy on the chair to his left, when his knees finally give out. Atany lands on his lap. They both laugh.

"I've been waiting for that for so long," she tells him with a smile.

"So have I," he replies with the same smile. They fall back into a long, hard kiss as they grind their bodies together, engaging in mock sex.

Beep, beep, beep. The console on the desk chimes.

"Captain?" Fental's voice fills the room. "Professor Hawking?"

The sounds snap them out of their moment. Realizing what just happened, she gets off Hawking's lap and walks quickly to the desk.

"Atany here," she says into the console.

"Is everything all right?" Fental asks with concern.

"Yes, fine, why do you ask?" she answers hastily.

"You and Professor Hawking were supposed to be in engineering with us five minutes ago."

"Holy shit," she replies, trying to hold back the embarrassment. "We're on our way." The two kiss one more time and hurriedly head out the door.

Chapter 7

Captain's log, stardate 30088.08. We are en route to the coordinates provided to us by Professor Hawking from his translation of the Forzak artifacts. In the meantime, Hawking, Fental, Benjamin, Diana, and I are trying to interpret, implement, and install the Forzak components while Ahijah and Bakkiah work on the possible properties of the vortex. We have four point five days to complete this.

The doors to the engine room open with a whoosh as Atany and Hawking enter the room. The doors whoosh closed behind them.

"Sorry we're late," the captain says. "We were unavoidably delayed."

"No problem, Captain," Fental responds.

"We're still trying to figure out where to begin," Benjamin continues.

"I can help with that," Hawking says as he lifts the three padds in his hand for the rest to see. "These are my translations of the installation instructions. Everything on the descriptions of the components has been removed so we can focus on the assembly exclusively." He hands a padd to Benjamin and one to Fental. He keeps the third.

"I suggest we start with the universal plasma phase converter," Hawking suggests. "That's where the power input terminals are. We have to configure an adapter unit."

"Then let's bring the unit over to that EPS manifold." He points to a conduit protruding from the forward bulkhead of the engine room.

The two men carry the component to the conduit. The half-meter-diameter conduit protrudes from the wall, at floor level, for four meters. It connects to a vertical conduit, again a half meter in diameter, that stands one and a half meters tall. They put the unit on the floor beside the conduit.

"Benjamin, Diana, find a way to power up that component," orders Atany as she turns to Hawking and Fental.

"Captain," Fental starts, "we need to get a work detail in spacesuits out on the deflector dish to install the deflector frequency modulator controllers. Those units should tie in with relative ease, but we should get them on ASAP."

"Okay," she answers, "get security and the spacefold drive technicians out there getting that done. See to it."

"On it," she says as she walks away and out of the engine room. Atany turns and walks over to Hawking.

"We need to fabricate two stands," he tells the captain.

"Why's that?" She looks puzzled.

"The universal plasma phase converter will sit on top of the EPS conduit," he explains. "When that's in place, we'll need to connect the system operations control unit, which will need a support stand, and the plasma intermix amplifier chamber, which will need a support stand.

"I see your point, Professor," she says as the two head off to the damage control supply room. That is where they will find the material needed to fabricate the stands.

While they are out of engineering, Benjamin and Diana begin fabricating the adaptor needed to attach the universal plasma phase converter to the EPS manifold. Using spare components for the matter/antimatter reaction chamber and parts from the spare articulation frame, they are able to construct a workable adaptor.

When Atany and Hawking return to engineering with the support stands just over an hour later, they find Benjamin and Diana tightening the last of the support clamps on the phase converter.

"Ah, Captain, Professor," Benjamin says as he looks up at them, "your arrival is quite timely."

"I see that," Atany says as they approach the engineers. "Are you ready to connect the system operations control unit and plasma intermix amplifier chamber?"

"As ready as we'll ever be," Benjamin responds.

"Good," Atany replies. "Let's get this job done." She slyly looks over at Hawking and greets his roving eyes with a sexy grin.

"I agree with the captain," he says as he picks up one side of the stand designed for the intermix amplifier. Atany grabs the other side.

As they set the stand legs on either side of the EPS conduit, Diana sets the stand in place for Benjamin, who has the system operations control unit in his hands. He sets the unit on the stand and slides the unit closer to the phase converter. He locks the two couplers together while Diana holds the stand steady.

Atany and Hawking lift the amplifier chamber into place, and while balancing the unit on its stand, they connect the couplings to complete the link. It takes several more seconds to be sure the whole assembly is sturdy.

"What's next, Professor?" Diana asks.

"I'm not sure yet," he responds. "Give me a minute and I'll figure it out." He lifts a padd and starts scrolling through the text.

"We need to run a power conduit from here to deflector control. That's where we need to set up the pre-fire cooling chamber."

"Before we assemble the conduit, we need to fire up the system so I can get a power reading," Benjamin says. "Having the conduit blow out is not something I would recommend. That would be not at all good."

"Right on," Atany replies. "I'd like to keep my ship in one piece."

"Do we have a measuring device that will handle that amount of power?" she asks Benjamin.

"I can use the warp field calibrator. It's the most powerful one we have. If we blow that, I can't build a strong enough conduit," he answers and turns to Diana. "Get the warp field calibrator."

"I'll be right back," she says as she leaves main engineering.

"I've got to check in on the bridge. You two men get that cooling chamber to deflector control. We'll meet back here."

The two men acknowledge as she heads out the door. They pick up the cooling chamber and make their way to deflector control.

The door opens, and the captain exits the turbolift, heading toward her command chair. She turns and heads toward Fental.

"Status," she commands.

"All decks report normal, Captain," comes from Roeton.

"Scanners are clear," reports Sacar, at tactical.

"Engineering reports warp engines running at ninety-seven percent but impulse at one hundred percent," Roeton finishes.

"Excellent," Atany replies as she approaches Fental. She leans in close. "Have you had a chance to review the data that Ahijah and Bakkiah are working on?"

"Briefly, while we were in Hawking's lab," she answers, then asks, "What are you concerned about?"

"I don't know," Atany admits. "I'm not sure." Her expression turns serious. "At this point, I should be concerned with the Rillians, Chandraka, and Horatha, but right now my biggest concern is this rift or vortex or whatever we call it."

"If you're looking for assurances, I can't give you any," Fental tells her captain.

"I don't know what I'm looking for. It's just that we're on the brink of bringing to life the greatest legend of the quadrant. I guess it might just be nerves."

"I hear ya. We're all by your side, Captain. Ahijah and Bakkiah know their shit. If they didn't, they wouldn't be here, correct?"

"Of course you're right," Atany says as she straightens her posture.

"I'll be in engineering in ten minutes. Let's get this mission finished." She turns and heads toward the turbolift. "Contact me there if anything changes."

The captain bypasses the turbolift and heads down the hall to the right. She goes past sickbay and goes into the mess hall, straight for the pot of fresh coffee. She leaves the mess hall with a large cup of coffee and a renewed outlook. She gets on the turbolift by the mess hall.

Atany walks into engineering, steam still rising from the cup in her hand. She blows lightly on the hot liquid then takes a sip. She walks up to Ensign Diana, who is connecting the warp field calibrator to the single half-meter-diameter coupler on the plasma intermix amplifier chamber.

"How's it going, ensign?" she asks.

"Almost connected, Captain," she replies. "I had to fabricate the connector, but I'll be ready in a few minutes."

"No worries, Ensign. Benjamin and Hawking aren't here yet, and we're not doing anything until they get back."

"Thanks, Captain," she answers. "I'll be ready when they get back." She returns to her work. The captain studies the three components set up in front of her. About five minutes go by.

"Finished," Diana says as she steps back from the assembly. Before she is able to take another breath, Benjamin and Hawking enter the engine room. The four congregate by the alien device.

"Next step?" Atany asks, focusing her attention to the two men.

"We've got to figure out how to power up these components and get a power output reading," Benjamin answers.

"The warp field calibrator is connected," Diana adds. "We just have to pray that the coupler I built can withstand the power."

"On that note," Hawking begins, "I need Benjamin to erect a level five containment field around this whole assembly, then I need the three of you to leave."

"What?" Atany asks, somewhat concerned.

"I don't expect any of you to risk your lives here. This has been my dream for as long as I can remember. You three run this ship. It's what you do. Don't put yourselves at risk," Hawking answers.

"With all due respect, Professor, I will make that decision, if you don't mind," she retorts.

"No disrespect intended, Captain. I am simply considering your safety."

"I appreciate that, Professor, but I am the boss."

"I'm sorry, Captain."

"No worries." She smiles slyly as their eyes lock for a moment. She continues, "Benjamin, you and Diana get that containment field up then get out. Professor, we will figure out how to power this up."

"Yes, Captain," comes from Benjamin and Diana as they walk away.

"Now that we're alone, I just want to say, I didn't mean to disrespect you. That's the last thing I—" Hawking says apologetically but is cut off.

"Ari," Atany starts while resting her hand lightly on his shoulder. "I really do appreciate your concern. That makes me more attracted to you, but I am the captain." She starts to giggle lightly. "I know you are usually in charge, but now I am." She kisses his cheek and, as she backs away, whispers to him, "You can make it up to me after we're finished here."

"You're on," he replies with a smile. A static-like sound fills the air as a translucent red haze from floor to ceiling surrounds them in an oval shape. Benjamin and Diana leave the room.

"Okay, Atany, let's get this done," Hawking says as he lifts and activates the padd in his hand, the padd with the translated operational protocols on it.

"We have to activate the universal plasma phase converter first," Hawking reads while Atany inspects the unit. "From the panel on the top of the unit," he finishes.

The panel on top has a row of lights running across the top part. Below them are five buttons, with indicator lights above them evenly spaced across the lower part.

"Well," Atany begins, "let me try this one." She pushes the button on the left side of the control panel on top of the unit. An indicator light above the button glows green, as does an indicator light and a digital indicator on the system operational control unit come to life, and a hum is heard in two of the three components.

"Hey, wait until I read what those buttons do," Hawking says.

"We're going to have to push them eventually. Starting from the left seemed logical," she defends.

"And what if they read from right to left?"

"Point taken, Ari," she says, "but since we are still here and since things lit up, I'm pretty sure I got it right."

"I agree, Dinema, but I'd rather we play it safe."

"Okay, Ari, but since we've gone this far . . ." She pushes the second button. The indicator above that button also glows green, and the row of indicator lights above the buttons glows lightly while the humming noise increases in pitch. An indicator light glows green, and a digital indicator activates on the control unit. They wait a few seconds.

"Well, so far so good," Atany says as she pushes the third button.

An indicator light activates on the plasma intermix amplifier chamber and above the button. Both are green. Another green indicator light, and the digital indicator comes to life on the system operational control unit.

"Excellent job," Hawking says to Atany as he scrolls down the content on the padd.

Atany pushes the fourth button. The light above comes on red. Neither of the two remaining indicator lights or the two digital indicators on the control unit lights up. Atany pushes the button again, and the red light goes out. She pushes it a third time, and the red glow returns.

"What the fuck!" she says aloud, annoyance in her voice.

"What's wrong?" he asks as he looks up and sees the red light. "Hang on," he says as he slows the scrolling speed on his padd.

"Almost there," he says reassuringly. "Got it." He inches down on the assembly instructions. "It'll turn green when the connection to the proper component is secure."

"So the first button I pushed turned on the system operations control unit. The second activated the universal plasma phase converter. The third turned on the plasma intermix amplifier chamber. So this fourth one must be for the pre-fire cooling chamber, which has yet to be connected," she explains in one quick breath.

"Exactly" is his only reply as the two walk to the front of the system operations control unit. This unit consists of five indicator lights evenly spaced across the top. There is a long rectangular section in the center of the panel. The upper square is a digital readout. Below that is a slide control with spaced lines from top to bottom.

There are two square panels on both sides of the rectangular panel.

Each panel has a digital indicator and a series of square buttons. Three of the indicator lights across the top are lit, as are the two upper square panels and the rectangular panel in the center.

"This one, in the center, according to the translations, is the plasma intermix amplifier chamber," Hawking says as he continues to read. "This slide control increases the power output." He touches the control.

"The units are active, so let me activate the warp field calibrator, and you can slowly raise the power level," she says as she makes her way to the other end of the assembly. By the time she finishes her sentence, her hand is on the activation switch; she turns it on. "All set," she says in what seems to be a single breath. "I'll monitor the power readings. Just go slow."

"So I guess you want me to raise the power level slowly?" he repeats sarcastically, with a smile. He slides the control handle up in small increments. As he pushes the slider up, the pitch of the hum begins to increase. The slider passes the fourth line, and the first green light on the universal plasma phase converter control panel glows brighter.

As the slider goes higher, the second green light grows brighter, then the third. The fourth light, now yellow, glows bright.

"What is our power level?" Hawking asks Atany.

"Just under half," she answers. "How far up is the slider?"

"Halfway, exactly," he answers.

"It looks like the power levels will be within tolerance," she observes.

"We have to go all the way to be sure. We don't want to be surprised by an expediential increase on the high end. That would suck."

"Yeah it would," she concurs.

Hawking brings the slider to the three-quarter mark, and the fifth indicator, the second in red, is glowing brightly. The pitch of the hum has also been increasing but is still not uncomfortable for the captain and professor.

"Where's the slider, Ari?" Atany asks above the sound of the hum.

"Seventy-five percent," he replies.

"Okay then, if anything bad is going to happen, it will be from now until full power."

"Don't worry," he says with reassurance. "I'll go slowly." They laugh.

As the slider reaches the top and the final red indicator light glows bright red, the humming sound peaks out and stays steady. The power level indicator peaks out at one hundred percent.

"We're at full power, Dinema. What's the power output level?"

"Output is at ninety-nine point five. We can handle the power."

"Most excellent," Hawking says excitedly.

"Right on," Atany agrees.

Hawking slides the lever back down to zero, and the hum decreases and the indicator lights on the control panel diminish. Atany moves to the universal plasma phase converter and presses the buttons in reverse order, and the devices shut down.

"Atany to bridge," she says in her now open communicator.

"Bridge here."

"Have Benjamin and Diana come down to engineering and disengage this containment field."

"Right away, Captain." The channel goes dead, and she puts her communicator away.

Two minutes later, Benjamin and Diana enter the engine room and go straight to the computer control panel, and within seconds, the hazy red curtain surrounding the assembly disappears with the familiar static discharge sound. The two engineers walk over to where Atany and Hawking are standing.

"We were monitoring the test from the physics lab," Benjamin says.

"I'll get the precise readings from the warp field calibrator, and we can start fabricating the power conduit to the pre-fire cooling chamber," Diana adds and walks over to the unit.

"Contact me when you get the conduit assembled and connected," Atany orders Benjamin.

"I'll call you as soon as we're done," he assures her.

"Right on," Atany responds and lightly slaps Hawking's arm with the back of her hand to get his attention. Hawking places his hand gently on the small of her back, and the two leave the engine room.

The doors open, and the first thing Hawking sees is the wall-size window directly in front of him, on the far wall. From that window he sees the streaking stars as the ship flies at warp speed. Looking down, outside of the window, he sees the bridge, then the front of the ship. Below the window is a huge bed, Atany's bed.

The captain leads Hawking into the room, and the door whooshes closed behind them. Hawking walks about halfway into the room and stops to admire the view.

"Breathtaking view, isn't it?" she asks as she steps in front of him.

"Absolutely," he says as he looks her over from head to toe and back up again. He takes a deep breath and smiles. "Yeah, and the stars outside are pretty amazing as well."

She steps in close, and their mouths slam together hard, without warning. Both start moaning seductively as their tongues rub against each other. Their bodies press hard together.

Hawking helps Dinema out of her uniform as she helps him out of his clothes. The view of this beautiful Utorian wearing only a black lace thong and glistening metal studs shining in the starlight, through both nipples of her supple breasts, makes him crazy with desire.

Hawking pulls her in tight and kisses her again. As their tongues caress, he slides his right hand down her spine, lightly guiding his fingertips along the middle of her back, until he reaches the crevasse between her firm ass cheeks.

He slides his open hand over her entire left cheek, and when his fingertips reach the top of her thigh, he stops. He squeezes her ass cheek firmly, with authority, with control.

Keeping a tight grip on her ass, he guides her in the direction of the bed. The back of her legs hit the bed, and they fall onto it. Hawking lands on top of Dinema, and she guides his body between her legs, locking her legs around his waist. They fall back into another long, deep kiss, moaning with uncontrollable passion.

Hawking slides his tongue gently down Atany's neck until he reaches her ear. Breathing heavy in her ear, he caresses her earlobe with his tongue, bringing it into his mouth. He gently slides her earlobe in and out of his mouth, causing her to moan deeply as her back arches slightly with pleasure.

Hawking slides his left hand up to her right breast and wraps his hand around it, gently cupping the fleshy, soft mound. As he squeezes the supple breast, he runs his lips down her neck in a trail of gentle kisses. By the third pulsing squeeze, his lips make contact with her erect nipple, flicking the metal stud with his tongue.

Atany moans loudly as his nostrils catch the scent of her pheromones. His head starts spinning wildly out of control as his brain registers the aroma.

"By the gods," he says between gasps of air. "You are so intoxicating, so addictive."

"Thank you," she says softly, seductively, as she pulls his head up and locks her lips on his, ramming her tongue as far down his throat as she could, grinding her hot, wet pussy against his hard, throbbing cock.

Finishing the kiss, Hawking runs the tip of his tongue down Atany's neck, continuing between her breasts as he slides his body down along hers. He stops his tongue at her navel and playfully darts it in and out. Her body reacts to the sensitive touch, arousing her even more.

When her moans subside, he continues to run his tongue down her belly until he hits the smoothly shaven tip of her clit. He rubs her clit with his lips as he slips his finger inside her wet, hot pussy.

Atany moans wildly with pleasure as he slides his finger in and out of her, and his lips and tongue work their magic on her clit. In less than two minutes, her body quivers in orgasmic ecstasy. He continues harder and faster, bringing her higher and higher. She screams loudly as her body erupts, sending waves of pleasure through her entire being.

"Oh fuck," she moans. "Oh, shit, that feels so good." After a thirty-second continuous orgasm, her body relaxes, but her breathing is heavy and labored; a huge smile spreads across her face. Aristotle takes hold of her thong panties with both hands and roughly slides them off her.

She quivers with excitement at his show of force, knowing he would not hurt her. He looks up at her naked body lying spread-eagle in front of him and can no longer contain himself. He takes his underwear off, exposing his throbbing manhood to the captain. Her eyes and smile widen with excited anticipation.

"Are you ready for more?" he asks her as he lowers his body, bringing his face inches from her burning crotch, her smell floating in the air, in his head.

"Are you kidding me?" is her reply as his tongue and finger go back to work, and her eyes roll up in her head as she starts to slip back into bliss, reaching orgasm three more times.

Hawking starts to run his tongue back up Atany's belly, to her navel, darting in and out a few more times, making her giggle. As he reaches her breast and slips her studded nipple into his mouth, he gets on his knees, pulling her pussy closer to him.

Letting go of her nipple, he pulls her hair firmly from behind, arching her head back. He locks his lips onto hers as he thrusts his large, hard cock into her wet pussy.

Atany moans loudly as he starts to penetrate her. Her moans grow even louder as he slides deeper in. Once fully inside her, he grinds his pelvis into hers, rubbing into her clit at the same time.

Dinema locks her legs around Hawking's waist and starts to slide her pussy along his rock-hard shaft, creating her own rhythm. She continues until she has two more orgasms. She lets herself rest.

He looks deep into her eyes and kisses her passionately. He looks into her eyes again.

"Now it's my turn," he tells her as he grabs her right leg and brings it up along his side. He puts her shin in the notch in his shoulder and grabs her left ass cheek firmly. He starts thrusting his cock deep in and out of her pussy. It only took seconds before Atany starts to moan again, the sound of exhaustion evident. This excites Hawking more.

He continues with the gentle pounding of Atany's wet, inviting pussy, keeping the same rhythm until she cums, then changing it, making her cum again and again.

During her fourth orgasm, the muscles in Hawking's body start to tighten with his impending orgasm. As the muscles deep inside Atany's pussy constrict around Hawking's cock and her body explodes, once again, in orgasmic ecstasy, his body explodes, releasing his fluids deep inside her. When she feels his release, her body explodes at a level she has never known.

They lay, with him on top, their bodies shaking from the release of such a vast amount of sexual energy, for about thirty seconds. He rolls to her side, wrapping her in his arms.

"That was so much more awesome than I imagined it would be," she says to him, with her beautiful smile filling the room.

"I was going to say the same thing." He smiles back. "You were magnificent, incredible."

"Thank you," she says as she closes her eyes and drifts off to sleep. He follows suit and, within a few minutes, joins her in restful slumber.

"Yes?" Atany asks after the intercom beeps.

"Benjamin here, Captain. The power conduit to the pre-fire cooling chamber is complete. We are currently connecting the cooling chamber to the deflector frequency modulation controllers. We should be done in about fifteen minutes.

"Excellent," Atany says. "I'll let Hawking know, and we'll be there as soon as possible. Out." She deactivates the intercom. She gets up from the chair at her desk and walks to her bed.

Atany slaps Hawking's foot playfully as she walks to the head. "We've got to go to work," she says as she kisses him long and hard. "Get up and get ready," she continues.

"I'll jump in the shower," he answers as he gets out of bed. "Give me five minutes please."

"I'll join you," she says, showing her amazingly beautiful smile. They head into the shower.

Chapter 8

*Captain's log, stardate 30096.91. The Forzak com-
ponents have been installed and we are preparing
for a full power test. We have stopped in a region
void of any celestial bodies in the event something
should go wrong. I pray to the gods that nothing goes
wrong.*

A tany sits at the head of the conference table. Present at this meet-
ing are Fental and Hawking, both sitting to the right of the captain. To her left is Lieutenant Commander Benjamin. To his left
are Ensigns Ahijah and Bakkiah.

"Before we fire up this device, I need to know what we can
expect," the captain starts. "Ahijah, Bakkiah, what has your research
come up with?"

"Well, Captain," Ahijah begins, "we've concluded that we have
a limited conclusion." Everyone looks confused. "All we've been able
to determine is that a vortex will open, allowing us access to a region
of space beyond our normal realm. Once we enter this vortex, a program installed in the system operations control unit will guide us to
the Forzak home world."

"You call that limited?" Benjamin asks.

"What we can't tell you," Bakkiah interjects, "is if the radiation producing this vortex is hazardous to our life forms, our ship. Or will the gravitational riptides within the vortex tear us to shreds?"

"I can see the significance of those answers," Benjamin replies.

"How can we put those issues to rest?" Atany throws out to the crew.

"I have a suggestion, Captain," Fental tells her.

"Okay, Fental, the floor is yours," comes from the captain.

"If you and the professor slowly increase the power output while Ahijah and Bakkiah monitor the sensor readings from the physics lab, I will do the same from the bridge. We'll do it all on an open channel."

"I would suggest no more than seventy-five percent power," Ahijah recommends, and Bakkiah agrees instantly.

Atany looks around the room, and all heads nod in agreement.

"Unless there are any other ideas?" Atany half asks as she starts to stand from her seat. The room remains quiet.

"Benjamin," Atany focuses attention to the chief engineer. "I want you to monitor all of the ship's systems from the bridge while we're doing this."

"Will do, Captain," he responds.

"Get to your posts," Atany commands. "We start in exactly five minutes."

Everyone leaves the observation lounge hurriedly.

Five minutes later finds Ahijah and Bakkiah at the computer terminals in the physics lab. Fental and Benjamin are at their respective positions on the bridge. Hawking and Atany are in main engineering, at the alien device.

"Are you ready, Professor?" Atany asks as her hand slides toward the control panel of the universal plasma phase converter.

"Would it matter if I wasn't?" he asks her with a smile.

"No," she replies nonchalantly as she pushes the first button.

Like the first time, when the button is pushed, the indicator lights and digital indicator come on. Atany pushes the second, then the third, with the same results. She mockingly hesitates when she moves her finger to the fourth button.

The digital indicator and the two indicator lights come on when Atany pushes the fourth button. Within a second, the power conduit starts to hum and glow as the energy that the alien components produce flows through it.

As Dinema pushes the fifth button, the green lights and lighted panel come to life. She makes her way to the system operations control unit and joins Hawking, who is glaring at the lighted console, padd in hand.

"Ready to power up?" Atany asks.

"Absolutely," he replies. "Just give the word."

Atany flips open her communicator.

"Fental here, Captain," the disembodied voice of the science officer is heard above the hum of power. "Are you ready?"

"Physics lab here, we're ready," Ahijah's voice joins in.

"Yes, we are. Keep the channel open, and let us know what's going on."

Atany looks at Hawking. "Begin," she says.

He starts sliding the lever slowly upward on the panel. The pitch of the hum and the indicator light steadily climb. The power conduit starts glowing brighter.

"Twenty-five percent," Hawking informs everyone.

"Readings unchanged," Fental reports.

"Same here," Ahijah also reports.

Hawking continues cautiously. "Fifty percent," comes from Hawking.

"I'm reading an unstable energy field forming five hundred thousand kilometers forward," Fental reports.

"Sensors reading an unknown energy generating from the center of the anomaly," Ahijah says. "Computers are analyzing the data as we speak. Right now there is no danger that we can see."

"Increasing power output to seventy-five percent!" Hawking shouts. "Seventy-five percent!" he shouts again after a few seconds.

"Energy field has stopped at a two-hundred-meter diameter, but the power inside the field is building."

"The fabric of space inside the vortex is distorting," Ahijah adds.

"Radiation output is nominal," Bakkiah interjects.

"We are still well within safety limits," Benjamin informs.

"We'll keep the power level here for a few more seconds so the computer can gather more data, then we'll power down."

"Captain," Bakkiah cuts in, "since we are in no danger, why not go full power and enter the vortex now?"

"No . . . we can't," Hawking says quickly, sternly. "If we go in now and the program kicks in, we may be lost since we are not at the required coordinates."

"Did you get all that?" Atany asks.

"Yes, Captain," Bakkiah says.

"All right then, we're powering down now." Hawking slowly slides the control lever down.

Atany pushes the button on the universal plasma phase converter control panel from left to right, allowing all the power in the conduits to bleed out into space.

"Observation lounge in twenty minutes," Atany says, and all acknowledge. "Bridge, get us back on course to the coordinates provided by Professor Hawking."

"Yes, Captain," comes from the bridge. "Back en route now."

Twenty minutes pass and all parties are sitting at the conference table in the observation lounge, exactly where they were previously.

"What have you got for me?" Atany asks all.

"The vortex stayed open at two hundred meters. The power readings went off the charts within the anomaly, but the outer edge remained at the same levels recorded before the anomaly formed," Fental reports.

"The fabric of space/time within the vortex began to reconstitute into something unknown to any science," Bakkiah adds.

"The radiation output was zero even when the unit was at seventy-five percent," Ahijah adds.

"That's not possible," Fental says as she looks at her padd quickly. "Everything emits radiation," she finishes.

"Everything that we know of," Ahijah responds. "Either this vortex draws the radiation back into itself or the type of radiation it emits can't be read by our equipment."

"During the test, all ship's system were at peak performance," Benjamin states. "The ship was, and still is, in perfect order."

"So when we get to the coordinates, we can activate the Forzak device and enter the vortex with no worries?" Atany asks.

Everyone agrees that the captain's summation is correct. She stands and all follow.

"Everyone back to duty stations," she says. "We have about four days before we arrive at the coordinates. Benjamin, get me more speed. Anything to get us there faster would be appreciated."

"We'll get on it first thing, Captain."

Everyone leaves except Atany.

An hour's passing finds all duty personnel at their stations. All ship's departments have reported normal. As Atany is sitting in her seat, going over the department reports, the intercom light on her armrest lights up.

"Atany here," she says after she activates the unit.

"Benjamin here, Captain, we have increased engine performance by eighteen percent. Increase speed cautiously."

"Right on, Benjamin. Good job," she says with a smile then deactivates the intercom.

"Helm," Atany continues, "increase speed in increments slowly."

"Aye, Captain," Lieutenant Merah says.

"Hold us at warp five," she continues.

Five seconds later, he replies, "Captain, holding us at warp five puts the engines in the red."

"Understood," she answers. "Maintain warp five."

"Yes, Captain," he replies.

"Captain?" Benjamin's voice sounds through the bridge.

"What is it?" she asks after she activates her intercom control.

"We need to slow down, Captain. My indicators are in the red."

"You need to find a way to get the indicators down, but we are not slowing down," she says with authority.

"Understood, we'll do our best."

"No. You'll get it done," she says again.

"We'll get it done, Captain."

She deactivates the intercom. "Let me know when your indicators go back in the green," she tells the helmsman.

"Will do, Captain," he answers.

The ship travels at warp five for forty-five minutes. There is nothing unusual going on. Atany signs the final status report on the padd in her hand. She looks up and focuses her attention on the viewscreen.

"What is the condition of my engines?" Atany asks.

"We are three percent in the red, Captain, down eight percent from your last check," Merah answers.

"Awesome. Benjamin's getting stuff done down there. What is our current ETA?"

"Three days, two hours," he replies.

She sits back in her seat with a smile slowly spreading across her face.

The ship rocks violently and lists to the left. From the viewscreen, everyone can see that the ship is spinning wildly out of control. There is no notice, no warning.

"What the fuck!" the captain shouts. "Report!"

"Warp engines offline," Merah reports.

Atany hits the intercom button. "Benjamin, what did you do to my engines?" she yells into her armrest.

"Nothing, Captain," he yells back. "The issue is external."

"External?" she repeats inquisitively. "Tactical, what, or who, the hell is out there?"

"I can't get a fix," Korah replies. "We're moving too erratically."

"Helm, get us under control."

"Working on it, Captain," Merah states as his hands glide over the controls, keying in commands as fast as he can. It takes thirty seconds before the image on the viewscreen becomes a static star pattern.

"Tactical, what's out there?" Atany asks again when she sees that the ship has stopped spinning.

"Reading a distortion one thousand kilometers off the port bow."

"Horatha!" Atany says out loud. "Lock torpedoes on that distortion and fire at will."

"Firing forward torpedo bays. Aft weapons offline."

"Continuous firing of all available weapons authorized."

"Firing all weapons."

The weapons barrage went on for nearly a minute. During the fire fight, the *Heaven* was rocked twice by enemy fire. Lieutenant Korah ceases fire.

"Enemy ship is veering off at one half impulse," he says.

"Damage on their starboard nacelle. It is venting plasma," Fental says.

"Venting plasma," the captain repeats. "On screen, now."

The ship turns to face the direction of the distortion. On the viewscreen, a small patch of shifting space is in the center of the screen. Within the small patch, to the right side, glowing red gas is spewing from nowhere.

"Can we pursue?" Atany requests.

"Yes, Captain," Merah answers. "Impulse engines still online."

"Full impulse. Intercept course," the captain orders.

"Yes, ma'am." Merah keys in controls. "Done." The ship begins its pursuit of the red gas.

"All weapons systems back online," Korah says after fifteen minutes of pursuit.

Atany leans forward in her seat, interlocking her fingers on her lap, elbows on the armrest of her chair. "Are we in weapons range?" she asks.

"Five seconds," he replies.

"When we are in range, fire all weapons. Don't stop until that ship is obliterated," Atany says coldly.

"Captain?" Fental questions her captain's command.

"This mission is too important. We cannot give anyone a chance to intercept us and take control of the Forzak device," Atany explains.

"We have damaged them badly," Fental begins. "They have already sent out a subspace message, and reinforcements are, undoubtedly, on their way."

"Your point?" Annoyance in her voice.

"They are disabled. To kill them like this is unjustified, without honor."

"You're right, Fental," Dinema says after a moment of reflection. "Tactical, when in range, lock onto the point of the plasma stream and fire two torpedoes. I want to destroy the nacelle, nothing more. Their approaching ships will be busy with them."

"Torpedoes locked on target," Korah says as he keys in more commands. "Firing two torpedoes." The torpedoes appear at the bottom of the viewscreen. Leaving a thin trail of plasma from their engines, they can be seen approaching the origin of the red vapor.

It takes six seconds for the torpedoes to hit their target. The first blast knocks out the shield generator, revealing the portion of the ship exposed by the missing shields. The second torpedo detonates on the nacelle, blowing it into three pieces. Two pieces fly away from both ships. The third piece, connected to the primary hull by sections of the support pylons, bends and strikes the shields protecting the hull.

The shields start to glow at the point of contact and shortly overload from the extreme pressure of the nacelle. The shield drops, and another section of the Horatha ship is visible. Explosions on several decks can be seen. The bridge crew stares at the viewscreen for several seconds.

"Engineering," Atany says into her intercom.

"Yes, Captain," Benjamin replies.

"How are my warp engines?"

"I need thirty minutes."

"You have ten."

"I'll have them ready in ten."

"Thank you, out." She looks at Merah. "Get us back on course. Best possible speed."

"Yes, Captain," he answers as he complies.

The ship silently spins around and heads in the direction programmed in the computer. It speeds along at full impulse for ten minutes.

"Benjamin," Atany speaks into the intercom. "It's been ten minutes. Where is my warp drive?"

"Ready when you are, Captain," he replies. "And you can have warp six if you'd like."

"I'll make sure you get a bonus for that. Merah, warp six, now."

Merah sets the control, and the stars start to streak. "Warp six," Merah says. "ETA two days."

"Very good," Atany says as she stands. "I'm going to the mess hall. I'll be back soon." She heads off the bridge, past the turbolift.

Atany sits at the table in the corner, placing her tray down in front of her. She picks at the food in the plate, not bothering to eat any. Fental comes in and sits across from her, placing her cup of tea on the table, cradled in her hands.

"What's troubling you, Captain?"

"Is it that obvious?"

"Yes, it is. What is it?"

"The Horatha. I nearly destroyed that ship and everyone on board. What's even worse is that I wanted to destroy that ship." She looks down at her plate for a long second. "I've never lost my cool like that until Captain Jehovah died. Since then, and since the start of this mission, I've felt that the only way to proceed is to destroy the enemy, not cripple." Sorrow protruding from her words.

"The Rillians attacked us on Brantax, and to be honest, we were lucky to get out of there unscathed. When we encountered the Chandraka, same thing; they attacked us. It's been self-defense all along." Fental tries to reassure her.

"It's just . . . this mission is so damned important," Atany continues. "I think it's even more important that we find the Forzak first."

"I'm on the same page as you on that, Captain," Fental replies. "So is the rest of the crew." She sips her tea and looks Atany dead in the eye.

"Everyone on board, at least the ones I've spoken with, are quite impressed as to how smoothly and how quickly our mission is progressing. Everyone, including me, thought we would be out here for a very long time."

"Why?" she asks inquisitively. "No one trusted me when I took command of this mission?"

"No, that's not it at all," she says. "The Forzak Empire has been nothing more than a myth for a thousand years, and in the span of a couple of weeks, we are this close to finding them," she finishes by holding her hand up, extending her thumb and pointer finger out, leaving a tiny gap between them, smiling while doing so.

"You're right, Fental," she tells her with renewed vigor and a smile. "Of course, you're right. When I finish eating, I'm going back out to the bridge, and we are going to push this little bitch of a ship to its limits and get this mission done." She takes a forkful of food into her mouth.

Atany finishes eating in about ten minutes. After refilling her coffee cup, she and Fental leave the mess hall and head for the bridge, at the far end of the deck.

"Engineering," Atany says into the armrest intercom.

"Benjamin here." His voice comes through.

"I want warp eight in thirty minutes, no excuses, thirty minutes," her voice booming with authority. "That's all." She sits back in her command chair, observing her crew.

Chapter 9

Captain's log, stardate 30099.07. Thanks to the efforts of Lieutenant Commander Benjamin and the engineering staff, we have arrived at the designated coordinates. We are preparing to engage to Forzak device. I pray to the gods that this is not a one-way trip.

"All hands, this is the captain." Atany's voice echoes through each deck, each room, as she speaks into her communicator. "We are preparing to activate the Forzak device. Continue to be vigilant at your posts until we're on the other side. Out." She holds her communicator open, keeping the channel open, and looks up at Hawking.

"Ready?" she asks. He acknowledges, and she activates the five buttons on the universal plasma phase converter. The system operations control unit comes to life. The three components start humming.

Hawking looks over the separate panels and ensures the devices are within operational parameters. He slowly slides the control lever up. The power blasts down the conduit, causing it to glow increasingly brighter. The pitch of the hum increases as the power increases.

"Twenty-five percent," Hawking says aloud.

"No change in ship's status," Benjamin reports in first.

"All as before," Ahijah's voice announces.

"Sensors showing nothing," Fental answers.

"Fifty percent," Hawking says after a few seconds. There is no danger alert.

"Seventy-five percent," comes a few seconds later.

"Vortex is forming exactly like the test," Fental informs Atany.

"Still no radiation, no danger," Ahijah says.

"Ship systems are still normal," Benjamin adds.

"We're at one hundred percent," Hawking says. A few seconds pass.

"The power level within the vortex has stabilized, Captain," Fental finally breaks the silence. "Its diameter remains constant."

"There is zero percent radiation output," Ahijah reports.

"Gravity readings within the vortex are well within ship's tolerance," Bakkiah adds. "But I must remind you, Captain, though the readings say that everything is good, there is no telling what's going to happen to us once we enter the vortex."

"Thanks for that reminder. Helm, bring us into the vortex, thrusters only," Atany orders.

"Yes, Captain," Lieutenant Levi's voice acknowledges. "We will be entering the vortex in one minute and twenty-two seconds."

"I see," the captain says. "In that case, hold our position here until I get up there." She takes a few steps back from Professor Hawking.

"I need to get to the bridge," she tells him. "I need you to stay here and monitor these components until Benjamin gets here. Once he does, meet me on the bridge."

"I'll be there as soon as I can," he answers as she walks away.

Atany steps off the turbolift and takes her seat. She looks around. "Benjamin, get down to engineering and monitor the Forzak components. Hawking needs to be here."

"On my way," he says as he stands and heads to the turbolift.

"Helm, bring us in," the captain orders.

"Full thrusters aye, Captain," Levi answers. "ETA one minute, twenty seconds."

The ship travels slowly toward the vortex. On the viewscreen, the image of the vortex starts to get larger, encompassing the entire screen in just over a minute.

"Vortex boundary penetrated," Levi informs the captain.

The turbolift door opens, and Hawking comes onto the bridge, walking to the side of Atany's chair, his eyes never leaving the black, empty void on the screen.

Atany looks up at him. "We just entered the vortex," she tells him.

"How deep is it?" he asks without looking away. Atany turns to Fental.

"Sensors are not reading anything," Fental says after several seconds. "Our sensor beams are being absorbed. There are no signals coming back to read," she finishes.

"Fental," Atany asks, "how far back is our entry point?"

"Unable to determine," she answers. "Signals not returning."

"Are you able to determine if the vortex is still open?"

"Not at all," Fental replies.

Atany turns slightly to the right. "Tactical, do your targeting sensors read anything?"

"No," Lieutenant Sacar answers. "There is nothing out there that I can read. No ships, no asteroids, meteors, comets, planets, nothing."

"So we are totally engulfed?" Hawking asks.

"That is what I said," Fental answers with a slight, sarcastic attitude.

"The program in the operations control unit should take over soon," Hawking says. "We just have to wait until it does."

"What do we do until then?" Levi, at helm, interjects.

"We explore," Atany says. "Levi, full impulse. Just keep us in a straight line."

He nods and keys in commands on his panel.

"Are we moving?" Atany asks after a few seconds.

"Unknown," Fental reports with a sound of slight confusion.

"My sensors can't tell," Sacar adds.

"Instruments show we are moving at full impulse," Levi says. "But since we have no frame of reference, I can't tell how far we've traveled.

"The computer calculates one point five million kilometers."

"Okay, then, we just sit back and wait," Atany says as she sits back, getting comfortable. Five minutes pass. Her comfort is short-lived.

The red alert klaxon blares without warning. Everyone is startled.

"Report!" the captain yells above the alarm.

"Nothing here, Captain," Sacar reports.

"I'm actually getting readings," Fental says. "Give me a minute to analyze."

"So am I!" Levi shouts. "Helm control is automatically being programmed by an external source."

"It's the Forzak computer program," Hawking says loudly.

"Sacar, shut that klaxon off now," Atany says, and the noise is silenced.

"Levi, let the computer run the program." A few seconds pass.

"Fental, what's happening out there?"

"It seems the vortex is closing in around us," Fental answers. "The power buildup around the ship has increased by thirty-eight percent."

"The external pressure is still well under our safety limits," Ahijah adds.

"We are still not reading any radiation," Bakkiah volunteers.

"The chemical composition of the vortex is changing," Fental says with amazement.

"What does that mean?" Atany questions her science officer. "How is that even possible?"

"I don't know, and I don't know," Fental replies. "I've never come across this before. No one has ever encountered this before. The data we've collected will keep our scientists busy for years."

All the bridge personnel are looking at their monitors, making sure all the data is being stored properly. Hawking is looking around.

"Holy crap!" Hawking says after his eyes lock back onto the screen. Everyone looks at him and, when seeing his face, turn their attentions to the viewscreen.

The screen shows that the empty void they are in has now become a sphere of pulsating beams of multicolored lights coming from the outer edge of the screen and curving into the center, which is becoming a spinning whirlpool of light.

Ten seconds pass when the spinning whirlpool of light appears to be expanding. It slowly grows in size. When the pool fills half of the screen, the center shows a forming circle of calmness, increasing in size a little faster than the outer edge.

It takes another twenty seconds before stars become visible in the growing circle of calm. Everyone on the bridge notice the stars nearly simultaneously.

"Start scanning that opening!" Atany shouts with excitement.

"I'm on it," Fental replies as she swings her seat to face her monitor, and she starts scanning.

It takes about thirty seconds for the outer whirlpool of light to engulf the main viewscreen. Another twenty seconds pass and the circle of calm envelops the viewscreen, showing normal space outside.

"All stop," Atany orders. "Where are we?"

Everyone spins to their monitors. Before anyone can speak, the ship rocks violently from left to right. The feel of a torpedo impact vibrates through the hull. A second torpedo hits, then a third. Lights flash on and off as panels on different consoles explode from power surges.

"What the fuck happened!" Atany screams in surprise and anger, her voice having to rise above the red alert klaxon and the sounds of plasma venting from torn conduits and exploding circuits. "Report!"

"We've been hit by three photon torpedoes!" Fental yells out her report. "Energy signature shows it is Horatha!"

"Horatha!" she repeats with more anger in her voice. "How the hell did they get here? What's going on?" Frustration joining the anger in her voice.

"Sensors show two ships off our starboard bow," Sacar tells the captain.

Confusion, frustration, and anger now distort the captain's beauty. She takes a deep, stern breath and straightens up. "I want to know what the fuck is going on now." Her voice is loud above the current ambient noise but calmly spoken. "Who has information for me?" Atany yells in a manner daring someone, anyone, to answer.

"Sensors showing the lead ship is Horatha. The design is similar to the ship that previously attacked us. Their shields are down, and they've sustained minor damage," Sacar answers the captain's challenge.

"Second ship is an Alliance assault transport. They're attacking the Horatha," he finishes.

"Roeton, hail that alliance ship," Atany orders, slightly calmer.

"I have the captain," he answers after a few seconds.

"On screen," she says, and in half a heartbeat, there is a redhead lieutenant on the viewscreen. Both Fental and Atany smile as their eyes widen in recognition.

"This is Lieutenant Daniel of the Alliance ship *Deliverance*. I will be more than happy to fill you in as soon as we get rid of the Horatha."

"Tactical!" Atany screams, momentarily ignoring the figure on the screen. "Lock everything you can muster and blow those fuckers away."

The screen changes back to the outside view. On the screen, the Horatha ship streaks to the left followed by the Alliance ship. The transport fires phasers at the Horatha, and the beams impact the aft shields.

"Firing all forward weapons," Sacar says as two torpedoes appear from the bottom of the screen, arcing to intercept the lead ship. The phaser beams blast out from the bottom of the screen, in a straight line leading just ahead of the same ship.

The phasers make impact with the enemy ship's forward shield just behind the bridge, or what Atany thinks is the bridge. The torpedoes make impact in the same spot. The first torpedo from the view from the *Heaven* makes impact on the shield while the second torpedo tears through the hull.

The transport fires two phasers. They miss wildly. Two torpedoes shoot from the rear of the Horatha battleship. Rather than lock on to the transport stalking them, they veer off in a long arc.

"Track those torpedoes," Atany commands.

"On screen," Sacar says as a curved blue line emanates from the front of each torpedo, completing the arc and leading right to the *Heaven*!

"Intercept those torpedoes!" Atany says with some panic in her voice.

"Firing phasers," he states.

"Phasers missed, Captain," Fental adds.

"Brace for impact!" Atany shouts. The ship rocks hard to starboard. The second torpedo makes impact, and the ship rocks more violently, the screen showing them in a slow, flat spin.

"Damage report!"

"We have hull breaches on decks one, three, and four," Roeton reports.

"Seven crewmen are unaccounted for. Deck one is unable to support life. The only power available are the batteries. Phaser banks and shields are down. Torpedoes are still online."

"Fire all torpedoes as we come into range."

"Firing," Sacar answers as six torpedoes fire from the forward tubes in a staggered formation. The six torpedoes race toward their target, seconds ticking by slowly. As the torpedoes disappear from view, two unknown objects appear in their place.

"Sensors identify the two objects as torpedoes!" Fental shouts.

"Hold on!" Atany yells as the torpedoes hit their mark. The ship, once again, is bathed in absolute darkness. The emergency lights come on, and all essential rooms are bathed in dim red light.

Atany, along with the rest of the bridge crew, see the six torpedoes fired by the *Heaven* hit the Horatha ship. The detonations are followed by a huge, brilliant explosion as the ship is obliterated. The Alliance transport flies through the massive explosion and slows. The main viewscreen goes blank as the wall panel to the left of the screen explodes in a brilliant shower of sparks and arcing electricity.

"Does anything on this ship still work?" Atany asks with apprehension and some panic.

"External communications are down, but internal system is operational," Lieutenant Roeton reports first.

"All tactical systems are down," Lieutenant Sacar says next.

"Helm control and navigation are shot to shit, Captain," Levi says. "We are not going anywhere soon," he adds.

"All sensors are offline," Fental starts. "Internal power is completely down. All that's left are battery packs, and they're at forty-five percent. Most of the available power is being used to maintain life support and atmosphere control."

"Suggestions?" Atany asks, looking around at her bridge crew. In that moment, a faint hum is heard in front of the blank viewscreen. The humming gets louder as three silhouettes of blue sparkles appear. In two seconds, three Alliance officers are on Atany's bridge.

Two of the officers head off to different stations on the bridge with equipment they brought over with them.

"Hello, Atany," the officer in charge says to the captain with a smile.

Atany smiles back, her eyes wide with excitement. They approach each other, embracing tightly and kissing slowly, longingly.

Hawking looks at them with added confusion.

"Hey, Danny," she replies as she takes a few steps back. Then, without warning, she bursts out in a fit of laughter.

Lieutenant Daniel looks at her with a look of curiosity. Fental starts laughing out loud, and that's when Daniel sees her.

"Fental?" he half asks in disbelief. "It is you. I didn't know you were here." He walks over to her, giving her a hug and slow, sensual kiss.

Hawking gets up from his seat and walks over to Atany. Daniel does the same.

"Daniel, this is Professor Aristotle Hawking." Atany points to the professor. "Ari, this is Daniel, my husband."

"I-I-I . . ." Hawking tries to speak.

"I've heard a lot about you, Professor." The tall, strawberry-blond lieutenant puts his hand out in greeting.

"Nice to meet you, Daniel." They shake hands.

"What are you doing here?" she asks Daniel.

"Right now I've got several crewmembers helping out in engineering and a couple helping out in sickbay," he answers.

"No, no," she says, waving her right hand. "You, the Horatha, out here with us, wherever 'here' is."

"After getting a status report from the professor's associates on Brantax, the Alliance decided to send us to find you, covertly," he starts to explain. "I didn't think we would ever find you, but we intercepted a disaster beacon from the Horatha ship you nearly destroyed. When we arrived, two ships were assisting. One set out to find you, and we flew into their blind spot, in their wake, to trail them. The other ship was too busy to notice our little ship. We arrived at the vortex as you were going in, and when the Horatha followed you in, we came with them."

"Very nice work," she replies, still smiling. "Very nice."

Reality comes back, and everyone finds something to repair.

"Long-range sensors detected a star system about two light-years from here. We'll get your ship patched up enough to get you there."

"We need to get the main computer and main sensor array back online first," Atany commands. "Despite what happens to this ship, we need to collect as much data about this place as possible. That star system may contain the Forzak homeworld."

"Engineering, when can we get some power?" the captain asks into her armrest.

"We'll have impulse power back up in five minutes, but, Captain, one impulse engine is destroyed," Benjamin says. "The warp coils in both nacelles are completely fried."

"Well, get us what power and propulsion you can as soon as possible. There is a star system two light-years from here that we need to get to."

"We'll get us there, Captain. I guarantee it," Benjamin says. The channel goes silent. Atany looks around at the smashed consoles and sporadic fires. Voices in the corridor tell of the enormity of the situation. She walks to the back of the bridge, past the turbolift.

Atany enters sickbay to find all the beds full, as well as the spaces on the floor between the beds. The two crewmen from the *Deliverance* are tending to the wounded.

"Where's the doctor?" Atany asks.

"In surgery," one crewman answers.

"How are things in here?"

"Serious, but it could be worse," answers the other crewman.

"Do you need help?"

"No," they both reply. "We can handle it."

"Right on," Atany answers. "And, thank you." She leaves sickbay and heads back to the bridge.

"Captain," Roeton says as she enters the bridge. "Benjamin reports we have impulse power. The port engine is ready, starboard engine inoperable."

"Good, good," Atany replies. "Levi, engage impulse drive. Let's see how she handles."

"Going to one-quarter impulse," Levi says as he keys in the proper commands.

The ship starts to move slowly, shaking under the strain. It takes about ten seconds for the ship to stop vibrating.

"Going to one-half impulse," he says aloud. The ship sluggishly picks up speed and starts to shake again. This time it took several seconds longer for the vibration to stop.

Lieutenant Daniel's communicator beeps. He takes it out. "Daniel here," he answers.

"Sir," the voice speaks, "the *Heaven* is moving."

"Yes, I know that," he replies. "Follow us, match our speed."

"Yes, sir," the channel closes, and Daniel puts his communicator away.

"Captain," Fental jumps in, "main sensors and navigational array are back online. We'll have the computer core rebooted in three minutes, then we'll be able to save the acquired data."

Atany acknowledges with a nod and a smile.

"Three-quarter impulse," Levi says as the ship starts to shake even more violently than the last time. The straining whine of the single engine reverberates through the ship. The vibration lasts for just over thirty seconds, thirty seconds that scared the shit out of everyone on the ship.

The viewscreen flickers on and off several times. By the fourth flick, it stays on. The stars are moving steadily on the screen for several seconds when the image freezes for a moment then starts again. The image does this several more times before stabilizing.

The viewscreen clarifies, and the image shows a brilliantly lit star in the center. On the left side of the glowing orb, closest to the ship and near the bottom of the screen, is a large barren rock. Behind the rock, and several million kilometers closer to the star, is a huge gas giant. There are several smaller rocks orbiting each other, to the right of the star. There is an unexplained eeriness in the scene.

"How long until we get there?" Atany asks.

"ETA seventeen minutes," Levi tells her.

"Maintain best speed," she replies.

Yes, ma'am," he responds.

The ship limps along slowly. The whining strain of the engine starts to soften as the engineers repair each of the damaged systems.

"Computer core has rebooted," Fental reports. "Data from the sensors is being analyzed. I should have some information about the system ahead in several minutes."

The time it takes for Fental to receive data seems like an eternity to those waiting.

"The star is a magnitude six," Fental begins. "Apart from the visible planets, there are three more on the far side. One has an atmosphere, a breathable atmosphere." Excitement flows from her words.

"Helm, set a course for that planet," Atany orders, and he complies.

"ETA to planet is nineteen minutes," he adds.

"Keep us safe and steady," she finishes.

"Hey, Atany," Daniel breaks the momentary silence. "I've got to get back to my ship. I'll be back when I can."

"Okay, Danny," she says and gives him another long kiss. "I love you."

"I love you too," he replies. "I'll see you soon." He walks to the spot he beamed in at, communicator out and open.

"Beam me over." He sparkles into nothingness.

Hawking walks over to Atany, who is sitting in her command chair. She looks up at him with a huge smile. She sees the confusion and sadness in his eyes and realizes his anguish.

"We'll talk when we can, I promise."

"All right," he says. "I'm looking forward to this."

As the ship passes the sun, the planets on the far side are visible. The two planets on the left are barren chunks of rock and ice, the one closest to the star being nearly the same size as the moon of Zareth. The second is slightly smaller than the first yet orbiting a bit farther out.

On the right side is a singular body, a glowing ball of blue and green, with patches of white. There is a single moon orbiting the planet, currently on its far side. The resemblance to Utoria is striking.

"Assume standard orbit," Atany tells Levi, and the ship, with all its damage, effortlessly glides into orbit, the *Deliverance* behind her.

"Benjamin, how long before warp power is back online?" she asks her armrest after activating the intercom.

"You're kidding, right, Captain?" he says with disbelief in his voice, nearly laughing at his commanding officer.

"What is that supposed to mean?" she asks, somewhat surprised at his demeanor. "Is something funny?"

"Captain, the matter/antimatter reaction chamber is destroyed," he explains. "The containment field generator for the antimatter storage pod is gone, literally. The last torpedo impact vaporized the unit. There is no way we can repair it without a month in dry dock."

"Understood," Atany answers as she sits back in her chair in silent contemplation.

"May I make a suggestion, Captain?" Hawking asks from the side of her chair.

She looks up and, upon seeing him, smiles the wide, beautiful smile that turns him on so much.

"Of course, Professor, what is it?"

"We need to go down there," he offers. "If this is the Forzak homeworld, then they must have technology to get us back, if not repair your ship."

"I haven't detected any life on the surface," Fental volunteers. "But I have located several large cities. We can beam down anytime."

"Really?" Atany questions with sarcasm. "Look around. Really?"

"Fental to transporter room," the science officer says into her intercom panel at her station.

"Transporter room here."

"Update repair status."

"Three pads operational, but just barely."

"My apologies, Dutona," Atany responds sympathetically. "I didn't mean to go off on you."

"No worries, Captain." Fental looks around. "I'm here too. I get it."

"Great. Let's go then," Atany says to Fental then turns to Hawking.

"Let's go, lover," she says softly, with a smile.

The three leave the bridge and, using the emergency ladder located behind the turbolift, carefully make their way down one deck. The shaft containing the ladder is, for the most part, undamaged. The danger here is not from debris but from darkness. With power being down so low, the shaft is bathed with periodic red lights, allowing anyone climbing to see the rungs in the wall but not much more.

The light that is supposed to light this shaft is supposed to come from the corridors of each deck. With available power being used to operate the necessary systems as well as the power automatically designated for the critical operational systems, there is minimal power available for lights. They must make their way in near darkness.

As Atany steps onto deck three , the only lights on are the red ones in the shaft. The three must make their way with hands on the wall. There is a dull light at the end of the hall, coming from the right. They round the corner to the right to find the door to the transporter room jammed open. The lights inside are at full power. Several voices are heard coming from inside.

The door at the end of the hall that opens into the airlock is gone. In fact, the entire airlock is gone. All that remains of that part of the ship is a barely functional forcefield. As the three enter the transporter room, the common thought is not of the Forzak home-world and the treasures it may hold but of the forcefield in the hall and how, if it fails now, all their efforts would be for nothing.

"Hello," Atany says to the three working on the transporter unit, trying to regain her focus. "Are you ready to send us down?"

"Ah, Captain, good news. We have another pad operational."

"Right on," she replies and, after a second, says, "Fental, get on the intercom and see if that lieutenant that came with us down to Brantax—"

"Abaddon," Fental reminds the captain.

"Yes, Abaddon. See if he is still alive. If he is, have him report here now," Atany continues.

"Will do," she replies and heads to the intercom panel on the wall.

"Hey, ah, Lieutenant?" Hawking asks the officer working closest to him.

"Urania," she informs him with a pleasant smile. "What's on your mind?"

"The forcefield covering that gaping hole in the hall. What is the possibility of it failing?"

"Not very," the battered officer answers. "As soon as it activated, the computer designated it as a critical system, so it will never be shut off by the computer, even if you try to enter a manual override code. It can only be deactivated if we lose all power. By the time it fails, it won't matter anyway."

Hawking seems to relax slightly after hearing her report. Fental comes back, and she's not in a more depressed mood.

"Good news, Captain," she reports. "Abaddon is still alive. He is on his way here. He's coming up from the shuttle bay."

It takes ten minutes, but Abaddon walks into the transporter room, a little battered but none the worse for wear. Fental hands him a phaser, communicator, and tricorder. The four step onto the transporter platform and position themselves on the circular pads.

Lieutenant Urania steps behind the control console and activates the unit. She slides the control levers downward in their slots, and the four people on the platform begin to dissolve into shimmering blue sparkles. The process takes several seconds longer due to the amount of damage the ship sustained.

The transport cycle finishes, and the four find themselves standing in the middle of a courtyard enclosed by three buildings. The architectural style of these buildings is unlike anything any of them have ever seen. The buildings appear to be organic, seemingly growing from the ground and curving up the way a vine climbs for the sun.

As the huge vine-like structures rise above the ground, bigger, evenly spaced, bulbous outgrowths appear. Each outgrowth has rows of openings, like windows. Some have a single row while others have multiple rows, leading the alien visitors to think the outgrowths are sections of interior space. Whether these are habitats or work areas is currently unknown. Atany, caught in the wonder of it all, takes a few steps forward, looking skyward at the buildings.

Beyond the buildings in front of them, the four can see a cityscape of similar-looking structures on the horizon. Though they appear to be far off in the distance, the impression the four get is of an extremely large metropolitan area, several times larger than any city any of them have ever seen.

With the exception of a few sporadic patches of trees, the entire horizon, in a full, 360 degrees, is lined by these buildings. From what they could see, it looks like they beamed down in the country.

After several seconds of admiration, three members of the away team take tricorders in hand and start taking readings. The sound of the three tricorders is the only sound, and the four are the only things moving anywhere. Atany walks over to Hawking. She stands in close, looking at his tricorder.

"Why didn't you tell me you're married?" he asks softly, solemnly.

"Would it have made a difference?"

"No, not from my perspective," he answers. "Not knowing that bit of info allowed me to start falling for you. I mean falling for you hard."

"I have serious feelings for you too, but I'm in love with Daniel." She takes a slight breath and, giving a little smile, continues, "But I still want you tonight."

"I can live with that," he tells her then changes the subject. "I have not detected any life of any kind. Not insect, animal, nothing flying, walking, or crawling. Only vegetation." His face showing his confusion.

"I'm reading an underground energy source. It is faint but present. Readings show a vast underground complex, some thirty kilometers in all directions, centralized from this location," Fental reports.

"I'm not reading any kind of radio signals," Abaddon reports. "There's nothing on any subspace channel. Nothing on conventional radio frequencies." He lets his tricorder fall to his side and looks around.

"This may sound strange, but I've got to ask," Abaddon continues. "If this is the Forzak homeworld and they've been extinct for a millennium, why are these grounds so well kept?"

"What are you talking about, Lieutenant?" the captain asks.

"Look around in this courtyard. The grass is well manicured, the structures are well maintained, yet our tricorders read no life. Who is maintaining everything?"

"He has a point, Captain," Fental defends.

"Thank you," Abaddon says sharply but politely.

"I think . . ." Hawking interjects. "All our answers can be found on the inside of these structures, somewhere."

"I concur," Atany adds. "Let's go." She starts walking to the building on the right. Not only is it the closest, but it has what appears to be a set of doors. The other three follow in close behind, cautiously looking around, just in case.

Atany and Hawking enter the alcove of the building cautiously, followed by Fental and Abaddon, all with phasers drawn and charged.

The captain pushes on the door, and it opens under a little pressure. They enter the building and fan out along the wall.

The foyer of this building is about forty meters in diameter and twenty meters high. There is a stairway that forms from the wall, spiraling up as it wraps around the inner wall until it opens into the first outgrowth.

The center of the room consists of a five-meter-diameter kiosk with eight consoles and monitors built into it. The four walk up and scan the device with their tricorders. It takes a few seconds to complete.

"It's a communications interface system," Fental informs. She starts keying in commands, and the console lights up and the monitor overhead flickers to life. The others gasp in fearful surprise.

"It's definitely the Forzak. That's now confirmed, Captain," Dutona says matter-of-factly.

"What are you doing, Fental?" Atany asks with some astonishment.

"We'll have to power this thing up eventually," she replies.

"Damn," Hawking says. "You're as bad as Dinema."

"Thanks," she replies. "I'll take that as a compliment," she continues, scanning the now powered-up unit.

Hawking does the same, followed by Atany. Abaddon soon follows along. Ten minutes pass while the four continue scanning and keying commands. Atany steps back and takes out her communicator.

"*Heaven*, come in, please," she says into the device. She receives silence as a response. She waits several seconds.

"*Heaven*, come in, please," she says again. A few seconds pass.

"Captain." A faint voice, covered in static, can be heard.

When Atany hears this, she adjusts a knob on her device. "*Heaven*, can you hear me?" she asks once again.

"Captain, your signal is better."

Now Atany can tell the voice coming through is Lieutenant Reuben. "What is the status on power?" she asks.

"Engineering reports impulse power at seventeen percent. Battery power is at nineteen percent."

"How is the main computer core?"

"Main computer is repaired and back online."

"Is there enough power to implement a continuous data stream?"

"From what we can determine, we can only if we devote all the communications arrays to the job. That means we'll not be able to contact you again," comes after a few seconds of silence.

"Understood," Atany acknowledges. "We have activated a Forzak computer interface. I want you to interface their computer with ours and upload as much of their database as you can."

"What happens if you run into a problem?" Reuben asks with concern.

"If we run into a problem, we'll contact the *Deliverance*," she advises.

"Very good, Captain. We'll begin immediately. We'll contact you when we've completed the upload."

"Excellent," Atany confirms. "Out." She closes her communicator. Her attention goes back to interface.

Ninety minutes go by as the four continue to access data as the *Heaven* uploads it. Everything is going along smoothly.

"Captain," Fental suddenly speaks up. "I found some data here that may be beneficial to our current dilemma."

"Explain," Atany instructs.

"Our ship is damaged beyond our ability to repair it, so we are stuck here. I've been scanning for data about this vortex device we have. I have found references to an immense battle cruiser far beyond anything we have. It is equipped with the device we need."

"Great news," Atany says. "But that was over a millennium ago."

"I don't think it was destroyed," Fental continues. "The last report in the log states the test run of the battle cruiser was postponed because of an unknown threat, unknown at that time. There are coordinates attached to this file."

"Captain," Hawking interjects, "if the unknown threat mentioned in the log is what wiped out the Forzak Empire, then the battle cruiser may still be at those coordinates."

"My thoughts exactly," Fental continues. "Our way home may be at those coordinates."

"Record the coordinates and keep them handy," Atany replies. "Right now we need to search this place. Maybe our scanning equipment can't pick up their signatures. Let's be sure." She turns to Abaddon. "How many levels down does this complex go?"

"Six levels down," he answers. "And nearly thirty up." He adds, "Though the ones above are very small, some of the rooms below are enormous." There is a long moment of silence.

"Fental, Abaddon, you take the upper levels. The professor and I will go down."

The others acknowledge. Fental and Abaddon head up the stairs, circling the room as they climb higher. They step onto the deck, and the room opens up before them.

The room encompasses the entire level and has three support columns in a triangular pattern. The stairway leading to the next level is about ten meters in front of them, continuing to spiral up. Along the remaining walls are about two dozen consoles and monitors. The glyphs that became so familiar on the crates that held the Forzak artifacts are imprinted in the walls above the monitors, spreading around the room, on every wall.

"Some kind of information center?" Abaddon asks Fental.

"I have no clue," she admits. "I couldn't even begin to guess what this place is for."

They move up to the next level, which is identical to the level below, just slightly but noticeably smaller.

They follow the stairs up the narrower, vertical corridor another twenty meters to a second outgrowth. They enter the lower level.

"Well, this is interesting," Fental says aloud.

Abaddon looks around to see the same thing he saw in the section below. Going up again, they find the second level identical to the one below.

"I see what you mean," Abaddon says.

They continue going up through four more sections before the stairway ends. Fental takes out her tricorder. She runs a scan and snarls in frustration, annoyed by the readings on the display.

"What's wrong?"

"This fucking tricorder is crap." She returns it to her side with force. "It knows that we are six hundred meters up, but that's it. Construction material, unknown; energy type, unknown; linguistics, unknown." She walks over to what appears to be a window and looks out, searching. "All I see out there are trees and buildings, that's it. No wildlife, no insect life, no people."

"Let's get back down to ground level," Abaddon suggests. "We can try another spire." He takes her gently by the arm to lead her down.

She shakes her head vigorously, like shaking out the cobwebs after a good night's sleep. "Maybe we'll find some answers in the next one," she confirms as she straightens up and starts walking down the stairs with purpose, Abaddon following.

In the meantime, Atany and Hawking find the stairway down located behind the base of the upward-spiraling stairs. They head down the tight spiral stairway, a stark contrast to the wider stairway going up. After going down some fifty meters, the two enter a huge room, nearly cavernous.

Inside this room is a series of structures, in rows and columns, running as far as the eye can see, forward and to the right. It is reminiscent of a generator room at a power plant, just much, much bigger. A cylindrical conduit runs up from each structure, angling so as to meet over the fifth column of structures and, from both directions, run to a larger, central conduit, which runs forward, in the direction they are walking.

"What do you think this is?" Atany asks, mesmerized by the size.

"Could be a generator room," Hawking speculates. "At least that's what it looks like. Let's take a walk down to the other end. That's the direction of those larger conduits running that way." He runs his finger in the air in the direction of the conduits. "When we find what those conduits connect to and what's inside of them, we may discover their purpose."

The two start walking to the far side of the room, which seemingly goes endlessly into the darkness. Hawking is keeping count of the number of structures in the closest row. It takes nearly three hours to walk far enough through this vast room to see the opposite wall.

As the two approach the end of the room, more of the far wall becomes visible. Forty more minutes pass before they realize there is a smaller room adjacent to this one. It takes another ten minutes of walking for them to realize the huge conduit runs into the smaller room.

By the time they reach the end of the row of structures, which Hawking now believes are energy collectors, drawing thermal energy from the planet's core and channeling it through the conduits, he has counted two hundred and fifty.

Atany and Hawking get to the entryway of the smaller room and stop in a moment of disbelief. The smaller room they are entering is large enough to house all the spaceships, of every class and configuration, from Utoria, at once.

This room is not only huge in width and length but also height and depth. After passing through a fifteen-meter-tall entry for twenty meters, they find themselves on what they can only describe as a catwalk. The ceiling of the room they are now in extends upward twenty meters, and the floor drops some sixty meters down.

In this huge opening is a square box. There are no marks or markings on it. There are no lights, hatches, or indicators on it. The only things they can see are three rows of one-and-a-half-meter diameter conduits, numbering in the thousands, running from the box into the walls, all the way around, above their heads.

The box is so huge that it can be touched from the catwalk, all the way around, or at least that's what they believe. It goes the full sixty meters to the floor and misses the ceiling by about a meter.

"What do you make of all this, Professor?" Atany asks in awe.

He tells her the theory he's been contemplating and continues, amazed, "This must be the power distribution unit. These conduits must go to all the buildings on the horizon." He points to the ones above their heads.

"These components are so massive, beyond anything I've ever comprehended," she admits.

"The power that went through these conduits must have been so great that we, most probably, couldn't even measure it," he adds and takes his tricorder out, scanning around in a full circle.

"Unbelievable," he says with some frustration in his voice.

"What's wrong?" she asks.

"These readings," he says. "Or should I say lack of readings."

"What do you mean?" Atany takes her tricorder in hand and starts to scan around her.

"There is nothing," Hawking tells her. "No power readings, no radiation output, unknown construction material, unknown construction age, absolutely nothing."

"Just like outside." She notices as she finishes her scan.

"We know that if your theory is correct, and these are for power, that they are working," she says. "The power for the interface in the lobby came from the planet, not our tricorders."

"You're right," he says. "Let's see if there are any other doors in this room," he says as he motions into the dark unknown.

She nods with a smile, and they start walking to the far end of the room.

The two walk another thirteen kilometers to find the far wall. They look around the corner of the blank box to see the catwalk extending, again, into a black void. They look at each other and shrug. They head off into the darkness again.

"I see the wall," Atany says, her words heavy as the walk around this massive box starts to take its toll. "At least, I hope it's the wall."

"It's still two and a half kilometers away," Hawking tells her.

"Yeah, but at least I can see it," she retorts.

They get to the corner and see the same thing as the last corner.

"Ari," Atany asks with inquisition. "I just noticed something. And it is very strange."

"What's that?" he asks.

"Look around and tell me what you see."

"I don't want to play right now."

"I'll make my point in a minute. What do you see?"

"Okay." He plays along anyway. "I see a huge box with conduits sticking out of it in two directions. What is your point?"

"That is my point." He looks confused, so she continues, "We're fifty meters below the planet's surface and forty-five kilometers, around two corners. Where's the light coming from?" Her smile grows huge and happy when his eyes grow wide and the lightbulb of revelation goes on in his head.

"Forzak technology," he says to her. "Almost seems like magic."

"The new technological advancements we'll have when we get back will take some getting used to," she replies with excitement, then, after several minutes, says, "That's enough of a rest. We've more exploring to do."

He agrees, and they walk on.

Six and a half hours later, Atany and Hawking emerge from the entryway under the spiraling staircase. They both shield their eyes from the sunlight that they haven't seen in nearly fourteen hours. It takes a few minutes. Fental and Abaddon are at the interface. They walk over.

"Welcome back, you two," Fental says. "Anything interesting down there?" she asks excitedly.

"A lot, a whole lot," Atany answers, still bewildered.

"It's huge," Hawking adds. "Huge beyond belief."

"Any word from the ship?" Atany asks Fental.

"No. I tried a few minutes ago and still no contact," she answers.

"They must still be uploading the database," she says.

"For fourteen hours?" Abaddon asks.

"The compatibility issues between the Forzak software and our own must be making the upload take a very long time. It will be worth it," Hawking explains.

"I'm hoping that's the case," Atany says. "Not a system problem."

"Fental," Atany continues, "contact the *Deliverance* and have them beam us up. We'll beam back to the *Heaven* from there.

"Right away, Captain," she says and walks some steps away to comply. In a few seconds, she rejoins the three and they sparkle away.

They rematerialize on the transporter platform of the *Deliverance*, with Daniel waiting there to greet them.

Atany runs down the few steps from the pad and gives Daniel a kiss, then gets back on the platform.

"I've got to get back to my ship," she tells him. "Stand by, I'll be in touch soon." She nods to the transporter operator.

Daniel smiles widely to Fental, who reciprocates. They sparkle away again, this time rematerializing on the battered platform of the *Heaven*.

The four make their way back to the bridge, carefully avoiding the debris and live power cables. It takes ten minutes to get from the transporter room to the bridge.

Chapter 10

tany and Fental take their positions while Hawking and Abaddon stand by her side. Fental inspects her station's operational status. Atany looks around at the devastation then activates her intercom.

"Benjamin, Dr. Anak, to the observation lounge, now," she says.

She stands and turns. She starts walking toward the observation lounge. "Fental, Hawking, you're with me. Everyone else, stand fast."

They get up and fall in behind her. Everyone else on the bridge stop their work, taking a much-needed rest yet looking puzzled at the captain's words.

The five are in the room in three minutes. Everyone is dirty, tired, and hungry. The captain looks at each of the four people sitting there.

"Casualty report, please, Doctor," she asks quietly, calmly.

"We lost nine. Five were blown into space," he begins. "Nine injured. Two are still in sickbay, one critical."

Atany stares at the floor. "Thank you, Doctor," she says softly then continues, "Benjamin, how's my ship?"

"I'm sorry, Captain," he says somberly.

"Just be straight," she says.

He understands. "Warp power is nonexistent. The matter/anti-matter reaction chamber was destroyed in the attack, as was the antimatter containment field generator," he begins as he scrolls down the list on his padd. "Impulse power is at thirty-three percent. There is no chance to get it any higher. Batteries are at twelve percent standby. Reaction control thrusters as well as the airlock on the starboard side are gone. Half of them on the port side are out as well. Spacefold drive is destroyed. Shuttlebay is also not repairable. All the shuttlecraft are damaged to some degree."

"What about the ex vees?" the captain asks with some dread.

"They are okay," Benjamin answers. "The problem is no place to land once they're launched."

The captain's hopeful smile fades but returns. "We have them if we need them. That's good," Atany responds.

"Transporters are down," Benjamin continues. "They are gone for good. It's only a matter of time before the systems fail. Environmental, life support, gravity control, inertial dampeners, they'll all fail, one at a time. There's no way we can repair the ship unless we go into dry dock. There's no other way."

The captain sits silent for a moment. "Fental, have you learned anything more about the prototype you told me about on the surface?" she asks after several long minutes.

"Yes, Captain," Fental starts with hopeful enthusiasm. "The battleship is huge, by our standards. It's three hundred and forty meters long. It stands twenty-two decks. The engines are capable of warp eight point five and has the vortex device already built in. It just hasn't been tested, and we don't know if it is even at the given coordinates."

"How long until we reach the coordinates?" she asks.

"We won't," Benjamin answers. "At least not in this ship. The coordinates are six point two light-years. It'll take this ship two and a quarter years, at our best speed, to get there."

"What about the *Deliverance*?" Hawking volunteers.

"Fental, you'll coordinate crew transfer with the *Deliverance*," Atany says, and Fental acknowledges.

"Did the upload complete?" Atany asks, and Fental answers, "We uploaded ninety percent of the database, the *Deliverance* uploaded the other ten percent," checking the padd in her hand.

"We'll have to scuttle this ship and bring everything to the *Deliverance*," Benjamin states, and Atany looks bewildered so he continues. "We have to disassemble the Forzak components as well as the computer core. We have to take all our operational technology."

"Why?" Hawking asks.

"For one thing, if another race makes it here and finds our technology and it's more advanced than theirs, we could, unwittingly, change the destiny of the region."

"That has a very familiar ring to it," Hawking says jokingly.

"What do you mean?" Benjamin asks.

"Isn't that what we're attempting to do?"

"No. I would have to believe the Forzak would not intentionally leave an active warship lying around for someone to find. No. What ended the Forzak civilization must have happened quickly, without warning. We are just abandoning her here."

"No, we're not," Atany says. "Remove the computer core and the Forzak components. Transport them to the *Deliverance*. When that's been done, have the remaining crew get their personal effects and transport over. Have Levi set the controls for the heart of the sun. The ship will be destroyed, and the pieces vaporized."

"We're looking at six hours, minimum," Benjamin says.

"Good," Atany says as she starts to get up. "I'll be in my quarters. I'll be back on the bridge in six hours. Let's get it done."

Everyone stands and head out.

"Oh, Professor," Atany says, "I still need to discuss a situation with you. Will you walk with me?"

"Of course," he replies as he walks over to her.

They leave the observation lounge together. Heading down the hall, they make their way to the shaft and climb the ladder up to deck one.

The only things left on deck 1 is the central corridor, leading to the front of the ship, two crew cabins on the port side, and the captain's and first officer's cabins. The majority of the starboard side crew quarters are gone, leaving just the starboard side bulkhead protecting the hall. The spots where the bulkhead had ruptured are protected by the hazy blue force field.

Atany and Hawking enter the captain's quarters. It's in disarray but intact. The door whooshes closed in an awkward manner. Hawking turns to see the door lock into place. He turns back to face Atany, who entered the room in front of him. He turns right into her arms, and their lips slam together in a kiss, more sensual than he's ever experienced.

She pulls him in tight as he places his hand on the back of her bare neck. Their lips press together even harder, their tongues dancing in delight. She lets out a moan that, in its eroticism, gets him semi-erect.

When she feels the start of his erection, she moans even more longingly. By the time her moan ends, he can smell her familiar scent, and his brain starts to spin and his knees buckle. They collapse on her bed, their bodies interlaced.

They peel off each other's clothes, slowly absorbing every second they are spending together, every touch and smell, every taste, sight, and sound. They lay naked on the bed, their cloths thrown around the room. The Forzak homeworld, visible from the window behind the bed, casts the only light in the room, bathing them in shadows.

Atany rolls on top of Hawking, straddling him at the waist. She takes his full erection between her thighs and gently, playfully strokes it up and down. She closes her eyes and focuses on the feel of his hard cock throbbing between her thighs, digging her nails into his chest.

Feeling himself approaching orgasm, Hawking grabs Atany, one ass cheek in each hand. He lifts her body off his erection and slides her up his chest. He brings her body down on top of his face, covering her clit with his lips. He slowly sucks her clit into his mouth and slides his tongue into its inner tip.

She starts moaning uncontrollably as every muscle in her body starts to tighten. As her thighs squeeze around Hawking's head, her hands grab fistfuls of hair, forcing his mouth deeper into her hot pussy. He fights off her hands, keeping a slight distance so his tongue can work her into orgasmic ecstasy.

He suddenly feels Atany's entire body start to spasm, very slight at first but steadily increasing. Within seconds, her whole body is quivering, and her moaning becomes loud and out of control.

Hawking starts sucking Atany's clit faster as he slips his finger into her now-burning pussy. She feels him enter her, and she bucks her hips up and down wildly as her body orgasms, spraying his face with her juices. He licks the area around her pussy of cum and starts to slowly run his tongue back into the folds of her clit.

He hears Atany moaning as she struggles to catch her breath. He runs the tip of his tongue from her clit to her belly button. As his tongue is traveling upward, he slips his finger into her soaked hole. Her hips start gyrating lightly.

As he slides his finger in and out of Atany, he continues running his tongue in between her breasts. Hawking's left hand wraps around Atany's right breast, squeezing gently. By the third squeeze, the tip of his tongue is circling her erect nipple, playfully flicking her shiny metal stud piercing her nipple. She starts bucking and moaning with no control, her fingers digging into the mattress. This orgasm is more intense and lasts longer the first one.

When her orgasm ends, Hawking stops his finger deep inside her, massaging her clit with his thumb while she catches her breath a bit.

"Oh, fuck, that feels good," she says softly as she gasps for air. Hawking stands up on the side of the bed. He starts sliding his finger inside of her while simultaneously rubbing her clit.

As she starts to gyrate again, Hawking gently guides her head, making her turn to the side. As she starts to moan, he slips his hard cock into her open mouth. She eagerly takes his large hard member into her throat. She slowly slides his cock in and out of her mouth, causing her to gag lightly.

Hawking once again feels himself ready to orgasm. He gently pulls his cock out of her mouth. She looks up at him, confused.

"What's wrong?" she asks. "Didn't it feel good? It felt smooth, nice in my mouth. You didn't like it?"

"That's not it at all," he replies gently. "I'm enjoying it too much. I don't want to cum in your mouth. I want to cum deep inside you while I'm fucking you."

She moans in delightful anticipation.

He bends over and kisses her hard as his finger, deep inside her, starts working its magic again. He maneuvers his body onto the bed, kneeling between her legs. He grabs a fistful of her hair with his left hand, gently cocking her head back.

Her cocked head allows Hawking to kiss Atany much deeper, and he takes advantage of that. Their tongues dance together, sensually rubbing against each other. He slides his finger out of her pussy and up to her clit, rubbing vigorously until she starts to gyrate her hips again.

When Hawking feels her gyrations beginning, he slides his hard, throbbing cock into her with authority. Her pussy clamps around his shaft and, even as wet as she is, grips his cock tightly but comfortably.

He picks up a rhythm and for twenty minutes causes Atany to orgasm two more times. Her body starts to build up for a third orgasm, and when Hawking feels this, his own body starts to constrict. For ten full minutes, they thrust into each other in perfect rhythm.

Dinema begins moaning frantically as she nears her third cock-slamming orgasm. As her body starts to convulse, Hawking begins to feel his orgasm coming to life. The two lovers orgasm simultaneously, moaning loudly while their lips are locked together. Their bodies, covered in sweat, lock together and intertwine so tightly they feel as one entity. Their orgasms gradually subside in unison.

They lay there, Hawking on top of Atany, his semi-hard erection still inside of her, kissing and moaning while trying to catch their breaths. He rolls off her and settles in by her side, scooping her in his arms.

"That was amazing," she tells him.

"You're amazing," he says.

"So are you," she replies.

"I've fallen in love with you, Dinema," he admits cautiously.

"But I'm married," she reminds him.

"I know," he says, somewhat disappointed, and kisses her deeply.

"I would never think to interfere with your marriage," he reassures her. "I still want you to know that." He takes a deep breath and continues, "You are everything I've ever wanted in a woman. I fell in love with you the moment I saw you. I'm still in love with you and will be long after I've drawn my parting breath. I'm in love with you on a level I've never experienced before."

"I don't know what to say. I wasn't expecting this to happen. I am more than smitten with you too, but we can't do this again."

"I know," he says. "Just know this, even after this mission, if you ever need anything, you just have to call. If I can, I will do whatever you need. Most importantly, I hope we will remain friends forever."

"That is something I can guarantee," she says with a smile. They fade off to sleep.

Atany and Hawking make their way onto the bridge right on time. Lieutenant Reuben is at the communications console, coordinating the scuttle. The rest of the deck is deserted with everyone working on the computer core.

"How's everything going?" Atany asks.

"Very well," he answers. "The Forzak components are already aboard the *Deliverance*. The computer core is almost disassembled. Everyone's personal effects and all nonessential personnel have been beamed over. We should be complete in fifteen minutes."

"Is everything ready here?"

"Yes, ma'am," he answers. "Levi, set the helm to automatically send the ship into the sun."

"What about the ex vees?"

"The pilots are assisting with the core disassembly. The ships are still in their cradles."

"Have the pilots report to their ships and prep for launch and have them launch when they're ready. We'll assist with the computer."

He complies with her order.

"They're on their way," Reuben tells her.

"Well then, let's head down and help with the core," Atany says, and the three leave the bridge. Atany stops by the turbolift and turns, taking one last look at the bridge. She joins the other three.

They make their way down the ladder to deck four. Coming from the ladder, they head down the short corridor and turn left, avoiding the piles of debris littering the hall. At the end, and on the left, of this hall is the port side computer core.

The three enter the core room to find Lieutenant Urania and Ensigns Ahijah and Bakkiah removing the last of the computer's memory rods and putting them in storage cases for transport.

"Almost finished?" Atany asks.

"Just about, Captain," Urania responds. These are the last of the memory rods. We'll be done in a few minutes."

"Outstanding," Atany says as they finish up.

Chapter 11

Captain's log, stardate 30110.01. I, with my crew, have transferred to the Deliverance. *I have sent the* Heaven *on its way to meet its fiery death in this strange star. We watched on the screen as it vaporized. We now head to find the Forzak battleship.*

"How long until we reach the coordinates?" Atany asks.

"About three minutes," Daniel says from behind her.

She spins around with a smile and gives him a long, slow kiss.

"Sensors picking up an object dead ahead, sir," the *Deliverance* tactical officer interrupts. "And it's big."

"Have Professor Hawking get up here," Atany says. Daniel orders it.

Hawking comes running onto the bridge, nearly out of breath.

"Are we there yet?" he asks.

"Visual in seven seconds."

Everyone on the bridge stares at the screen. The seven seconds take an eternity to pass.

In the center of the screen appears an object, not quite discernable, but there. The object grows larger as the seconds tick by.

Everyone stares, mesmerized by the image growing on the viewscreen, an image not seen in over a thousand years.

They see a long rectangular object floating vertically in space. Its lower third is wider, with two squares side by side. The upper third is only slightly larger than the center and cones to the end. There is a support pylon on each side of the center with a nacelle on each. There is also a hatch on this section big enough to put two of the assault transports they are in fore to aft with room to spare and three side by side.

As they approach closer, they see that the ship is made up of three sections connected by narrower connections. They see objects on the back side, expanding beyond the width of the ship.

"This is the bottom of the ship," tactical reports.

"I see it now," Daniel affirms. "Bring us around to zero, four, five mark zero, four, five."

The ship veers sharply to the right and straight up.

"Go to two, four, five mark zero, five, zero then adjust our attitude control to match that ship," Daniel orders.

The ship turns and rolls to offer our heroes a better view.

They approach the ship from above at a downward forty-five-degree angle. As the crew make out the image getting bigger on the screen, they stare in awe. The size and scope of the ship is mind boggling.

The nose is three decks tall and fifteen meters wide. There is a sheet of armor plating on each side, flaring outward ten meters on each side and five meters up and down, wrapping around that portion of the ship. The sheets are nearly two and a half times longer than the *Deliverance*.

Beyond the armor plating is a five-deck square connector sixty-five meters long. It is topped by a twenty-five-meter long three-deck-tall section that is topped by a fifteen-meter-long, two-deck-tall section. Behind these sections is a five-deck-tall, ten-meter-long section, seventy-five meters wide, extending thirteen meters beyond the port and starboard sides of the connector, looking like a *T*. The third section is about eighty meters long, flaring out about five meters on each side. It extends down two decks and up four. The top flares back five meters as it goes toward the back. This section is topped by a three-deck-tall, ten-meter-long section about eighty-five meters wide, extending beyond the hull slightly more than the one on the second section, making a slightly bigger letter *T*.

Adorning this section of the hull are two antennae arrays, one at each end. One is a curved rectangular array. The other is a flat square array of some kind of metallic mesh.

On each side of this section are support pylons. These pylons are twenty meters wide by sixty-five meters long. They are four decks tall.

Each one of these pylons has a nacelle-like structure on the end. They are five decks tall and one hundred and forty meters long but only five meters wide.

The fourth section of this massive ship is another connector, five decks square and twenty meters long. This one leads to the final section, easily identifiable as the drive section.

This part of the ship is a hundred meters long, extending fifteen meters wider on both sides, two decks up and one deck down. The section on top is slightly narrower than the main body but just as long. It stands five decks tall. Mounted on top of this, closer to the rear, is a ten-meter long, five-deck tall vertical connector. On top of this connector is a fifteen-meter long, four-deck-high section. This part is a hundred meters wide, forming the largest of the three *T*'s. On the back of this drive section are two square exhaust ports, each one capable of accepting the *Heaven* within its housing.

"That is one impressive fucking ship," Hawking says in awe after a long silence. The silence continues for a time.

"Any readings?" Daniel asks his tactical officer.

"Yes," he replies. "I need a minute to collate the data." Several minutes go by. Everyone is still in awe of the ship on the viewscreen. So in awe they don't notice Fental enter the bridge.

She comes up behind Atany, Daniel, and Hawking, looking at the padd in her hand. She stops on the side of Hawking. When she looks up to speak, she is entranced by the ship on the screen.

"Readings coming in," says tactical. "Wait, that can't be right."

"What is it?" Daniel asks.

"I'm not getting any readings. It like it's not there. There are no power signatures, but I see lights. I don't get it."

"Don't worry," Fental tells him, "we felt that way on the planet. Zero readings from a structure we were standing in."

"Send the ex vees ahead to make sure there are no surprises," Atany says.

Daniel turns to make it so.

"Please don't do that," Fental says, looking back at the padd in her hand, scrolling through quickly.

"Why not?" Daniel asks.

"That ship has an automated defensive system," she answers as she locates the instructions on the padd. "If we approach it, we'll be blown to dust."

"Then what the hell do we do?" Daniel asks.

"The vortex device has a program in it that will deactivate the first defensive level," Fental explains.

"Well, that's no problem. We installed it on this ship while you were on the planet in the event the battle cruiser didn't exist," Daniel tells them.

"Fantastic," Atany says with surprise. "Have you tested it yet?" she asks excitedly.

"We did a power test, and we are well within safety margins," Daniel answers, smiling at Atany's slight giddiness, as does Hawking.

"How's that?" she asks. "In an assault transport?"

"Alliance higher-ups decided the archangels needed a special ship," he says. "It may look like an assault transport, but we have a warp eight engine, extra shielding, and weapons. We're small, but we bite hard."

"Wow! I love it," she says with a laugh of excitement. "Professor, you and I need to activate the device."

"Let's do it," he says.

They start to leave the bridge when Atany turns. "Is the engine room in the same place?" she asks jokingly and leaves with Hawking.

The captain and professor enter the engine room and find the Forzak components connected to a conduit in the corner of the room. As they approach the alien devices for a second time, they stop and look at each other. They assume the positions they had when they did this on the *Heaven* two days earlier.

Atany pushes the buttons in sequence as Hawking monitors the system operations control unit. As before, the components activate as she pushes the buttons, the hum becoming evident. After pushing the fifth button, she joins Hawking, placing her hand firmly on his ass.

"How do we activate the program?" Atany asks.

"I don't know," he answers. "The last time it was automatic."

"Okay," Atany says after a few minutes of thought. "Bring the power to twenty-five percent." She calls Daniel on the bridge. "Can you bring us in closer? We think it may be proximity activated. Have the ex vees go in ahead. Hopefully, they can keep the defensive systems busy while we approach."

The four fighters pull ahead of the transport and shoot down in a huge arc to face the Forzak battleship head on. As they approach the monstrous vessel, the battleship comes to life. Lights start glowing sporadically through the ship. Four circular lights on the front of the two nacelle-like structures start to glow red.

Without warning, eight bolts of some type of plasma energy screams toward the fighters, four from each side.

"Evasive action!" Rigel screams to her comrades. The four ships peel off in different directions. The energy bolts fly in between them, heading off into space.

"At least they're not guided," Jullian, in Ex Vee Two, comments. The others agree as another volley of bolts shoot from the Forzak battleship, two bolts aimed at each ship.

"They can aim at us, though," Jasmine, in Ex Vee Four, says.

"That's not fair," Borkin, in Ex Vee Three, adds. Another volley of energy bolts launches at them.

"Evade the best you can," Rigel orders, and they all agree.

The four ships start zigzagging in and around the dozens of bolts now coming at them. Several close calls keep the pilots on the edge of their seats. The *Deliverance* approaches head-on while the weapons fire in directions away from them.

The system operations control panel starts to whine and hum softly as lights in its interface panel flick on and off. As quickly as the barrage started, it stops. The stillness gives the pilots a shutter. They circle around for another pass, and the massive battleship remains silent.

"I think the program worked," Rigel reports. "Assault is over. Battleship is quiet." As the fighters inspect the craft, things start to happen.

"There's activity," Jasmine tells everyone. "The hatch on the underside is opening. The power is coming on inside of the bay."

"That's great," Daniel says, somewhat more relaxed.

"Keep close," Atany says. "We're going to bring the *Deliverance* into the bay. Come in behind us."

"Copy that," Rigel answers, and the others acknowledge.

The *Deliverance* slowly approaches from the underside of the battleship, cautiously closing in on the opening. The ship stops directly under the open hatch.

"Tactical analysis," Daniel requests.

"Same as before, sir," is the report. "No readings. Nothing at all. Days like this suck."

"If we're not careful, this day may suck more," Daniel says. "Positive Z axis. One thousand k.p.h."

The ship slowly rises up into the hatch. The fighters come in after the *Deliverance*, in the same pattern, gently gliding into the compartment. The hatch closes behind them, trapping them inside.

The compartment they are in is four decks tall, with floor space capable of accommodating the five ships plus. As the outer hatch closes, another hatch closes in between the two center decks. The ships are above the closing hatch, confining them to a two-deck space. The second hatch closes fully, and the ships settle on its plating.

"Atmosphere report," Daniel commands.

"Sensors now reading an atmosphere and rising internal pressure," Fental, now at an available computer station, reports. "Readings equalizing. Pressure and atmosphere are identical to the planet. Environmental conditions spreading throughout the ship," she finishes.

"The ship is powering itself up?" Daniel half asks in confusion and admiration.

"That is what I said," she answers. "We can leave the ship anytime."

"Put me on intercom," Daniel tells his communications officer, who complies.

"This is Daniel. It is now safe to disembark the ship. Gather for instructions at the bottom of the landfall ramp, in front of the ship. Out."

The crew leave the ship and gather at its nose.

There are twenty-one crewmembers left from the *Heaven*, two are still in sickbay, each with a nurse, seventeen standing on the deck. With them are the four pilots and the seven members of the *Deliverance* crew, the archangels.

Atany, Hawking, and Daniel move to the front of the crowd.

"Hey, I need your attention, please," Atany says. It takes a minute for everyone to quiet down. Everyone focuses on the three.

"Listen up," she starts. "We have two primary goals right now. Find the bridge and find the engine room. Once that's done, we need to figure out how it all works then get this bitch home." Acknowledgments and cheers spread throughout the crowd.

The crowd splits into two groups. Lieutenant Commander Benjamin, Lieutenant Merari, and Ensign Diana, the *Heaven's* engineers, lead the first group. Captain Atany, Lieutenant Daniel, and Professor Hawking lead the second group.

Lieutenant Fental finds the door control unit, and after several minutes, she gets the huge heavy-looking door to open. The crew exits the hangar deck, fourteen going aft and fourteen going forward. It doesn't take long for the two groups to lose sight of each other.

"Any idea which way to go now?" Atany asks Hawking, who's looking at a padd.

The group is stopped at a four-way intersection. There is a door about ten meters down the hall in front of them. In both the port and starboard halls is the same thing, a door about fifteen meters down the halls.

"Give me a second, and I'll figure it out," he says, looking up. He looks at the three doors then looks back down at his padd.

"We go that way." He points at the door to the left.

Fental goes to the door ahead of the rest. She studies the door control, and after a few seconds, the door opens. The group goes through and sees the corridor ends after another ten meters. At the end of this corridor, another one runs left and right, from the front to the back of this ship.

The group led by Professor Hawking gets to the end of the corridor and turn right. They follow that corridor to the end and turn right, the only way they can go. There, fifteen meters down the corridor, is another door. Fental works on that door for several seconds, and when it opens, they find a two-meter-diameter, three-meter-tall capsule presumed to be a turbolift.

Fental and Hawking enter the capsule to inspect it, and once in, the door closes behind them. The two keep their composure and start to inspect the interior. On the wall to the right of the door is a large plaque with three rows of fifteen glyphs, similar to the ones on the artifact boxes and cave walls.

Hawking scrolls through the data on his padd, looking for a match to the symbols on the plaque. He shows annoyance after about three minutes and expresses it with a soft grunt.

"What's wrong, Professor?" she asks.

"None of the glyphs on the plaque are on this padd, and this padd has all the glyphs that we've recorded."

"These glyphs must be very specific combinations, for turbolift destinations perhaps?" she speculates. "And if that's the case, the one on the top should bring us to the top deck."

"Yes," Hawking says. "Good assumption, but which one is to what destination? I can't find any matches."

"There's only one way to find out," she says as she presses the top left glyph. The capsule starts moving in an upward motion. It comes to a stop after about thirty seconds. The capsule rotates to the left, ninety degrees, and the door opens.

The door opens to a corridor that goes on for five meters then turns sharply to the left. Fental presses the top right glyph. The door closes, and the capsule rotates one hundred and eighty degrees. The door opens to a mirror image. The corridor goes on for five meters then turns sharply to the right.

"Well, that's interesting," Fental says to Hawking, who silently agrees. She presses the center glyph. The door closes, and the capsule rotates ninety degrees to the left. The door opens to a room that makes both of them stand wide-eyed. They step out of the capsule, and the door closes behind them.

They turn away from the door and fully take in what they see. The room they are in is twenty-five meters square and four meters tall. On the far wall, where the main viewscreen should be, is a window. This window measures ten meters long and three meters tall. It is recessed into the inner bulkhead fifteen centimeters. Within that fifteen centimeter lip is a row of diodes going all the way around. On each side of the window are banks of computers that go all the way to the port and starboard side bulkheads, as well as the spaces on the top and bottom.

Along the portside bulkhead, from front to back, are roughly thirty computer terminals with ten seats starting from the back, evenly spaced, with the last one about ten meters from the front bulkhead. The starboard side is exactly the same. The back bulkhead is completely barren with the exception of the door the two came from and one door, five meters away, on each side of it.

Ten meters in front of Fental and Hawking are two seats facing the window. In front of those two seats and ten meters from the window is a long computer console with four seats. On both sides of that console and recessed into the floor are consoles with two seats each. Behind those consoles is another similar pair of consoles.

"This must be the bridge," Fental states.

"I would have to agree with that," Hawking says.

"The number of crew needed to man this ship must be in the hundreds," Fental says. "Way more than we have."

"We can only hope we can automate the bulk of the systems," he answers. "If not, we're up shit's creek."

The two walk to the two seats in the center. They each take a seat, inspecting the armrest interfaces.

"Not unlike our own setup," Fental compares.

"Yeah," Hawking agrees, "but not knowing what does what could be very dangerous. I'm going to try to find a match for some of these glyphs while we wait for the others."

"Good idea," she says as she stands. "I'm going to check out these other stations." She starts walking to the four-seated console five meters in front of her.

Hawking and Fental spin in surprise when the door they came from whooshes open. Atany and Daniel, along with several members of the bridge crew, step out. The door closes.

"Holy shit!" Atany says in awe.

"I know, right?" Hawking replies, smiling like a giddy schoolboy.

Atany walks over and sits on the side of Hawking. The rest of the group spread out and inspect the different stations.

In the meantime, it takes Lieutenant Merari about forty-five seconds to get the door at the end of the corridor open. The group goes through and turns right at the end. Here they encounter another door. Merari gets this door open to find another five meters ahead. He leaves the group and, approaching the door alone, gets it open.

When the second door opens, they see another door twenty meters down the corridor. In the center of that corridor section, on the left bulkhead, is a double door opening. This door looks stronger, more secure, than the ones they've passed through. Across from that door is a central corridor.

The group makes their way to the bigger doors while Merari gets to work. While he is trying to open this set, the others check down this new corridor, which doesn't take long. Though it is only slightly wider than the corridors they were just in, it has a door fifteen meters down. Along both bulkheads, from the junction to the door, are two rows of glyphs. They are in random groupings with gaps in between.

Ensign Diana records the glyphs on both walls with her tricorder while Merari opens the doors. It takes him several minutes to get these doors open because of extra security protocols. The doors open with a loud whoosh.

The group enters this room, and are all taken aback by what they see.

This room is the back section they saw from the outside. It is one hundred meters long, fifty meters wide, and eight decks high. There are six rows of cylindrical tanks, of different diameters, and all nearly the full eight decks tall, from the front to the two square units at the rear of the room.

The center of the room, from front to back, is a cleared passageway with computer terminals laid out sporadically down both sides. In the center of this passageway, even with the backside of the square units, is a singular console.

Interwoven between and around these tanks are miles of conduits connecting various tanks together. Also interwoven are catwalks and ladders, allowing access to all the sections of all the tanks.

Each of the square units at the end of the room is twenty meters square and twenty-five meters long. There are conduits running from the tanks into these two boxes. Along the inner wall of both of these boxes are rows of computer terminals and monitoring systems.

As the group walks toward the boxes, terminals and monitors flicker to life as the people walk by. As the first computers come to life, power travels to the next ones down the line ahead of the group. Lights come on above them, showing the full scope of where they are. Crewmembers stop at various terminals, examining the data coming up on the screens.

Lieutenant Commander Benjamin makes his way to the interface in the middle of the passageway. The glyphs appearing on the screen are a complete mystery to everyone in the group. Benjamin takes out the padd that Hawking gave him. He starts looking for matches with the glyphs appearing on the control interfaces. Others gather around to help.

Captain's log, supplemental. We have been on the Forzak battleship for six hours. Translation of the glyphs is slow but steady. Systems on the ship are slowly coming to life. Hopes are high that we can be home within a day.

"Do we have helm control yet?" Atany asks the three men sitting at the console in front of her.

"If I'm reading this correctly, we have control of the thrusters, but that's all," Levi answers.

"Let's test that," Atany challenges. "Fire up the thrusters, and let's see if we move."

"Right away," he says and manipulates the controls. Looking out of the window, everyone on the bridge can see the stars move out of position, indicating that the ship is, in fact, moving. Everyone cheers loudly.

"I have internal communications," Roeton says. "Benjamin is waiting on the line."

"Patch him in," she says.

"Captain, engineering here, the power started coming on when we got down here. We're making good headway figuring out these systems. I will contact you in an hour with an update."

"Right on," Atany says with excitement. "Keep up the good work." She looks around the room. "Any more good news?"

"Tactical systems are powering up," Sacar informs her. "Korah and I just need a little more time to get the hang of the controls."

"Keep on it," she replies.

"We've got several science stations available," Daniel tells her. "Don't ask us what anything means. Maybe when Benjamin is ready with his report, we'll have more data for you as well."

"Let's go, people!" Benjamin shouts at the group. "I told the captain we'd have more data in an hour. Don't make me a liar. If you think you know what the stations are for, say something."

The room remains quiet for a long while.

Diana walks up to Benjamin. "Come with me," she says. "I need your opinion."

They walk about halfway back to the entrance. Diana motions to several components. She points to one component specifically. "This looks very similar to the component that ran the vortex device. What do you think?" she asks.

"I think you've got a killer eye," he compliments her. "I think you are definitely right. Now let's see if we can find anything else that looks familiar." They walk off into the tangled mess of conduits and catwalks.

"Commander." The voice comes from somewhere in the room. Benjamin looks around but doesn't notice right away.

"Commander, over here." He looks around and sees a hand waving above the others' heads. He makes his way over to the Ensign Voltarus, the *Deliverance* engineer.

"What have you found, Ensign?" he asks.

"Voltarus, from the *Deliverance*," she answers. "I found what I think may be the warp field control computer." She shows him the glyphs on the interface and monitor.

He double checks her work carefully. "Damn good job, Ensign," he says. "See if you can figure out the operational protocols, then run several computer simulations. When you have the protocols down, call me over again."

"Will do," he answers.

Benjamin starts walking toward the control console in the middle of the central passageway. He stops at his console. "Hey, everyone, listen up!" he shouts, and in seconds, he has everyone's attention. "One of these control systems is for the navigational deflector array. We need to find that control panel."

Several minutes go by while everyone checks the monitors for any clues about the navigational deflector array.

"Found it!" A shout of excitement comes from inside the spaghetti-like maze of conduits and computers. "At least I think so."

Benjamin makes his way to the raised hand in the clutter. He looks over the glyphs on the screen, comparing them to the glyphs on his padd.

"Benjamin to bridge," he says into his communicator.

"Bridge here," Atany answers.

"We've located the power control unit for the navigational deflector array. I'm powering it up now, so when you locate the controls up there, you have power."

"Thank you," Atany says. "Keep up the good work down there."

He puts his communicator away and makes his way back to the console he was working on. He resumes the inspection he started earlier. It takes him several minutes to find the panel on the console that activates the controls in the various other panels. The activation of this particular console causes readings to change on other monitors. Everyone notices.

He continues working at the console for another thirty minutes. He finds a small panel on the upper right corner of the console. The panel has a single button in the bottom left corner with a light to its right. There is a small mesh screen above them. He pushes the button.

"Bridge here," Lieutenant Roeton answers.

"Engineering here," he says into the panel.

"Benjamin, it's the captain. How's it going down there?"

"Ah, Captain. We've isolated the vortex device and the warp drive sections. I've isolated what may be the main control unit. Identifying the components is kinda easy. Translating Forzak is the hard part."

"Keep me informed."

"Will do, Captain." He deactivates the intercom panel and continues trying to make sense of the glyphs on the screens.

Merari and Diana come over to him. "Commander," Merari starts. "We have determined that all these consoles are monitoring stations for all these tanks. All we need to do is determine which monitor goes to which tank."

"After we determine that," Diana interjects, "we need to figure out the difference between good and bad reading. After that, we'll be ready to bring the engines online."

"That's awesome," Benjamin replies happily. "Let me know when you have the glyphs figured out."

The two acknowledge and go to the console against the port side drive engine, at least that's what the engineers think it is.

"Captain!" Sacar shouts across the bridge. "Tactical is up and fully functional."

"Great," she responds. "Can you give me a threat assessment?"

"Absolutely," he answers as he gets to work. Several seconds pass. "Sensors show that the surrounding space is clear."

"That's even better," she replies. "Levi, how are you guys doing?"

"We've got the bulk of these controls worked out. Another hour and we'll have it all worked out." There is hesitation in his voice.

"But what, Lieutenant?" she asks sternly.

"We won't know how sensitive these controls are until we are in flight."

"Understood," she says with a smile. "I won't hold it against you."

"I've located the navigational deflector control," Ensign Torres, the helm officer from the *Deliverance*, says.

"Excellent," Atany answers. "Power it up."

"Aye, Captain," Torres replies and, after a few seconds, says, "Navigational deflector array is at full power. All systems showing normal."

"Captain," Merah, who is sitting in the seat second from the right, adds next, "I've identified this console as the spacefold drive." He motions to the panel on the end of the console. As he motions to the panel to the left, he continues, "This one is the vortex device."

"Excellent," Atany says with a smile.

"Science stations active," Fental tells Atany before she can ask.

"Another hour and we'll be able to link our tricorders to these stations, and the tricorders will translate the data," Daniel adds.

"Captain," a voice booms before she can comment on Daniel and Fental. A light on her armrest glows bright. She hits the button.

"Go ahead," she says.

"Anak here, Captain. We found sickbay two decks below you. Our patients are here. The nurses and I are trying to access the medical database and see what goodies we can find."

"Very good, Doctor. Keep me informed." She looks at Hawking, sitting on her right. "Great news all the way around." The glow of her smile dominates the room.

"At this rate, we should be home in a few hours," he replies.

"Benjamin to bridge," booms after forty-five minutes, sending a wave of panic through Atany, who's thinking the worst.

"Go ahead, Benjamin," she says.

"We've adopted several tricorders to assist with translation. We now know the various systems, but there are gaps."

"Such as?" she asks.

"Though we know everything is functioning properly, there are sixty-five storage tanks down here. All are on or about three quarters full. We've identified seven of them as part of the water reclamation system. We are assuming the rest are fuel, but we have no clue what type of fuel. Each tank has a glyph with a corresponding console, but we can't find any reference to type, chemical makeup, toxicity, nothing."

Hawking gives an exaggerated cringe, making Atany laugh, thinking about what's coming next. He is right.

"If everything is functioning properly, I'm guessing that you're ready for a power-up test?"

"Did you hear what I said, Captain?" he asks.

"Yes, I did. When you power up the engines, you can determine the danger while Levi gets used to the helm control. Power up on my mark."

"Engage," Atany says to both Levi and Benjamin.

"Bringing engines to one-quarter," Benjamin's voice sounds. Even through the intercom, the dull roar of the engines can be heard.

"Bringing helm to one-quarter impulse," Levi announces.

As Levi manipulates the controls, a change in the engines can be heard, straining under the force and millennium of deactivation. The stars on the screen start to move as the ship lurches forward. After about a minute, the strain on the engine starts to ease. The ship's vibration smoothes out. They continue for two minutes.

"Anything out of the ordinary?" Atany asks. Everyone answers no. "Bring engine power to one-half," she orders.

"Done," Benjamin answers as the engine roar gets slightly louder.

"Helm, one-half impulse."

"One-half impulse," Levi repeats and complies. "Done."

The stars move faster. Again, the straining of the engines and structural vibration subside, and it soon feels like the ship isn't even moving.

The ship streaks through the heavens, traveling at nearly 150,000 kilometers per second. The captain sits back in her seat, Hawking sitting in the seat next to her and her husband at a science station. Fifteen minutes pass without incident. She looks around the bridge then activates the intercom.

"Status report, all divisions," she orders.

"Engineering here." Benjamin responds first. "We have green lights across all boards."

"Helm control is one hundred percent," Levi says.

"Tactical reporting," Sacar says next. "All systems fully operational and showing no threats."

"Science stations all normal," Fental reports. "Analysis of the region shows nothing out of the ordinary."

"Communications show all frequencies clear. Transmitter and receiver units fully functional," Roeton reports.

"Okay then, bring engine power then helm to three-quarter impulse," Atany orders next.

"Engines at three-quarters," Benjamin informs the ship's crew.

"Helm to three-quarters," Levi says. "Done." He finishes, and as before, the engine strain and vibration, though less intense this time, take longer to subside. Another fifteen minutes go by.

"Full impulse," Atany orders, and after the engine strain and vibration subside, she lets another fifteen minutes go by.

"Status report, all decks," Atany orders once again.

"Engineering, all green."

"Helm, green."

"Science stations systems operating within parameters."

"Tactical, green."

"Communications, green."

"All the monitors over here are reading within parameters," Rigel volunteers to everyone, and Atany acknowledges.

"Helm, full stop," Atany commands.

"Full stop," Levi repeats and complies. The ship slows to a stop with the firing of the front maneuvering thrusters.

"Full stop," he repeats when the ship finally stops moving.

"Benjamin," Atany starts, "have you located any computer down there tied into the vortex device?"

"Yes, Captain, we found it a short while ago," he replies.

"Activate it," she tells him.

"Right away," he says, and in several seconds, the smaller individual sections on the vortex device panel come to life.

"Professor," Atany turns to Hawking, "you're up."

Hawking turns to her, nods, and stands. He walks over to Merah and taps on his shoulder. Merah looks up, and seeing Hawking there, he gets up and offers his seat. Hawking sits, and Merah sits in the seat on the end.

Hawking takes a few moments to familiarize himself with the controls. He starts manipulating the controls, and in less than a minute, a beam fires from the nose of the ship and begins to form the vortex. It takes several minutes for the vortex to stabilize.

"Fental?" Atany asks.

"Sensors show the vortex is the same configuration as the one that got us here, only larger," she replies.

"There is no identifiable radiation, no heat, nothing at all," Daniel adds.

"Is everyone ready to go home?" Atany asks the crew, and from both the intercom linked to engineering and the bridge, soft cheers are heard.

"Good," Atany says with a giggle. "So am I. Levi, take us in."

"Yes, ma'am," he says, smiling as he sets the controls. The ship starts moving forward, slowly closing the gap to the vortex.

Without warning, the beam leading to the vortex shuts down, and the vortex closes in on itself. A scream is heard over the intercom.

"Benjamin, what happened?" Atany asks.

"Unknown, Captain. I'm going to check," he says. Thirty seconds pass.

"Captain," Benjamin says nearly panicked, "it's Ensign Bakkiah, he's been murdered." Everyone on the bridge looks at the captain in shock.

"Details," Atany demands.

"His neck's been broken," Benjamin explains. "His head's been spun nearly all the way around."

"What happened to the vortex beam?" she asks next.

"I don't know," Benjamin answers. "I'll check the vortex device."

"Get Lieutenant Abaddon and Ensign Aurora to the intercom," she tells him. They answer her in seconds.

"I want the two of you to find out what happened to Bakkiah."

"We're on it, Captain," Aurora says.

"We'll take care of it," Abaddon answers her.

Atany looks around the bridge, noticing all eyes are on her. She looks at Fental and Daniel at the science stations.

"Daniel," Atany says softer, more composed, "will you and Torres go down to engineering and give Abaddon and Aurora a hand finding out what happened to Bakkiah."

"You got it, Dinema," Daniel replies as he stands. "Torres, you're with me."

"I'm with you, sir," Torres answers as he stands, and he walks to intercept Daniel on his way to the turbolift. They enter and the door closes.

Daniel and Torres enter the drive section and head straight to Benjamin, who is at the vortex device. He looks up in annoyance.

"How's the vortex device?" Daniel asks.

"The plasma intermix amplifier chamber is badly damaged, and the pre-fire cooling chamber is trash," Benjamin tells them.

"We need to speak to everyone. Can you gather them together, please?" Daniel asks.

He nods. "Everyone gather around!" Benjamin yells, and the size of the room amplifies his voice. Everyone gathers around close to the three.

"Everyone, look around at the people on the side of you," Daniel begins. "If you notice some who is not here now, who came here with you, give me their name."

Everyone looks around, muttering among themselves. It takes about a minute.

"Ensign Ahijah isn't here," comes from the small crowd.

"One of the crewmen from the *Deliverance* is missing!" another voice shouts.

Daniel looks around with concern.

"*Deliverance* crew, sound off!" he shouts.

"Voltarus," comes from the group as he steps into Daniel's view.

"Richards," is heard as he steps out and joins Voltarus.

"Peters, where are you?" Daniel asks and gets silence for a response. "Peters!" he shouts again, louder this time. Everyone looks around.

"Fan out," Daniel shouts. "Find these two now."

Everyone spreads out throughout the room. It only takes a few minutes before a shout is heard. Benjamin, Daniel, and Torres move toward the shout with others filing in behind them.

Rounding a very wide tank, they see his legs first, his body pushed up against the tank to keep the body out of view. It is Ensign Peters, murdered the same way as Bakkiah. A scream is heard across the massive room, and the three make their way there, followed by everyone else looking at Peter's lifeless corpse.

The three cross the span of the room and press their way through the onlookers. As they move around a console, they find Ahijah, her body clumped in a pile, wedged between some conduits and the computer console.

"Dr. Anak, Dr. Nire, report to the drive section. Now!" Daniel shouts into his communicator.

"We're on our way," Anak replies.

Daniel changes frequencies and continues, "Captain," he starts.

"Atany here. What's going on?"

"We have two more bodies down here."

"What!" she screams angrily. "I'm on my way."

Anak and Nire enter the drive section with Atany and Fental on their heels. They head directly to the crowd near the port bulkhead. As the four approach, a path is cleared. A final part in the crowd offers them the first look at Ahijah.

Anak makes his way to her side, slowly inspecting her body.

"Where's the other one?" Nire asks.

"Follow me," Daniel answers. "And, Doc, it's Peters," he tells Nire.

"Understood," Nire responds. The two walk across the room.

"Abaddon," Atany turns to the chief engineer. "Where's Bakkiah?"

"I'll show you," he replies. He raises an arm to point the way as they walk toward the starboard side engine. Abaddon and Aurora follow.

Atany kneels to inspect Bakkiah's body, careful not to disturb any evidence. She stays kneeling quietly for a few seconds. She stands and turns her attention to Abaddon and Aurora.

"Stay here with Bakkiah until the doctors arrive." They acknowledge as she turns to her engineer. "Show me the vortex device."

They walk away, heading toward to the components behind the second tank down. They walk past the tank and around the radius. They stop at two components mounted on a metal rack; both are damaged.

"What happened here?" she asks.

"Both components are severely damaged. Some kind of acid, I think. I've got to send people on a scouting mission to try to find replacement components. As soon as we find them and replace them, we can get out of here."

"Can we use the components that we have on the *Deliverance*?"

"I don't see why not," he replies. "That would save us a shitload of time." He thinks a minute more. "Yes, I think that'll work."

"Now, did anyone in here hear anything before Bakkiah's body was found?" Atany asks him.

"Not a thing, Captain," he answers. "Everything was going without a hitch. The vortex device indicator on the central control console went red, then I heard a scream, went over, and saw Bakkiah.

After contacting you and the *Deliverance* guys got here, we found two missing. We searched and found the other two."

Atany and Benjamin walk back to where Bakkiah's body is and see both doctors looking over the lifeless lump. She calls Daniel, Hawking, and Fental over to join them.

"How the fuck were they killed, Doctors?" Atany asks sternly yet softly.

"Their necks were broken, twisted so hard their necks snapped like dry tree limbs," Anak answers.

"Well, Benjamin, it looks like there is a murderer among your team," Atany tells him.

"And a saboteur," Daniel adds.

"How do we tell who it is?" Hawking asks.

"We should also consider that there may be more than one," Fental volunteers.

The metal conduit support, three inches to the left of Atany's head, suddenly explodes as a phased energy bolt strikes it. Atany drops to the floor. Two more energy bolts, fired from different directions, converge on the console protecting the captain.

Everyone standing with Atany hit the deck, trying to crawl behind some protection. The group of crewmembers scatters in different directions, hiding behind tanks and consoles.

"Stop shooting!" Atany screams. "Are you fucking idiots!" Two more bolts hit the computer in front of her, giving her the answer to her question.

"So you are fucking idiots!" she yells. "One wrong shot, and you'll destroy the ship!"

"We would rather destroy the ship than allow the Alliance to possess it!" the voice from behind a tank labeled *Water* shouts back.

"Who is *we*?" the captain asks as she pokes her head around the side of the console. The explosion of an energy bolt, inches from her head, makes Atany duck back behind the computer.

"That's not important, Captain!" the voice shouts back. "Just know that this ship will cross back into our space only under my command."

"That's not going to happen," she responds as a flash of light from her right catches her attention. She looks over to see Lieutenant Abaddon with an MX1903 assault phaser rifle.

"You know you're outmanned and outgunned. Where are you gonna go?" she yells at them while motioning for Abaddon to move behind the tanks and to get behind the sniper. He acknowledges and moves out.

"We're willing to die before letting you get this back," the voice says as Lieutenant Daniel makes his way along the portside bulkhead, quietly weaving under and around the maze of conduits. Across the room, Abaddon cautiously moves up.

"If you're planning on killing everyone, then what's the harm in telling us who employed you?" She peeks her head out slightly, and again, an energy bolt explodes inches away. She sits back behind cover, hoping Abaddon is able to see where the shooter is.

Abaddon crawls around several more tanks. He slowly peers around the tank. He sees the back of the shooter sticking out from behind a tank. He takes aim with his rifle, centering the scope on the back of the shadowed head.

"Tell me who sent you!" Atany screams in frustration. The shooter fires, and at the same time, so does Abaddon. The shadowed shooter slumps silently forward, never knowing what killed him. Daniel is now behind the last tank. He looks around it and sees the talker, rifle in hand.

"You'll have to beat it out of me," he replies.

Daniel makes his way around to the tank that the saboteur is using for cover. Abaddon makes his way to the body of the person he shot. It's Lieutenant Urania, one of the space-fold drive technicians. "I'll be damned," Abaddon says to himself. "Too bad, she was hot."

"It won't be me beating it out of you!" Atany shouts back.

"What's the matter? Ain't got the guts to do it yourself, Captain? Can't handle it?" the voice keeps taunting.

"I'd love to," Atany says back with all sincerity, "but my husband is closer."

"Yeah, bitch," the voice says. "Where is she?" He laughs mockingly.

The saboteur turns to his left and sees Abaddon. Raising the phaser rifle to his hip, he fires twice. "There you are, bitch!" he shouts as he shoots.

The first round hits Abaddon in the upper shoulder, sending him reeling backward. The second bolt hits him directly in the face, burning through his skull and instantly boiling his brain. He's dead before he hits the floor.

"No," Daniel says to the unknown crewman. "He's right here." He moves up to the saboteur and gives him a powerful front kick in the upper chest, knocking the rifle from his hand. He grunts in pain as he slams into a tank. Daniel spins his body completely around and, when he's come full circle, lifts his leg high in the air. The top of Daniel's foot slaps hard against the side of the saboteur's face.

Atany looks out from behind the console to see Daniel kick him in the face. Her eyes widen, and her jaw hangs open in disbelief.

"Holy shit!" Atany says. "Lieutenant Amariah? The fucking cook?" She steps out from behind the console. Other crewmembers stick their heads up one at a time after seeing the captain do it.

Daniel gives Amariah three quick jabs in the jaw. Quickly stepping back allows Amariah to miss the full force of the punches. Amariah then lets out a scream as he charges at Daniel. He bends lower as he rushes Daniel, burying his shoulder into Daniel's stomach. He continues pushing until Daniel slams, back first, into a large tank.

Daniel grabs Amariah's uniform tunic from the waist and pulls it over his head, momentarily pinning his arms. The next thing Amariah feels is Daniel's knee smashing into his gut, knocking the wind out of him. He feels a second, then a third.

Fighting for air and his head reeling from pain, Amariah wiggles out of his tunic and falls backward. Rolling over, he springs to one knee, his left arm across his abdomen. He looks up at Daniel.

"Now, like the lady asked, who paid you?" Daniel asks him.

"Fuck you," is his reply. He stands, brushing off the last attack. Both men take up a fighting stance as they slowly circle each other. The rest of the group starts to gather around.

Amariah slides forward while throwing several sidekicks, which Daniel blocks with his arms. With each kick, the gap between the men closes. On the fourth kick, Daniel holds Amariah's leg at the thigh. He leans in with two quick jabs to the face then sweeps his other leg, sending Amariah to the floor.

Daniel takes advantage by kneeling on the side of Amariah, still tightly gripping his thigh. Daniel's fist slams into Amariah's cheekbone four times, the force of each one increasing with each punch.

"Who hired you?" Daniel asks sternly. Silence is the answer.

Daniel's fist slams into Amariah's face with a fleshy thump.

"Who hired you?" he asks more sternly this time, and again, silence.

Daniel's fist slams into his face again; blood splatters from Amariah's nose, and his lip splits in two. Daniel takes a couple of deep breaths.

"Now, who hired you?" Daniel now screams at Amariah, who stares blankly back in defiance. Daniel slaps Amariah's face.

"Who hired you?" he yells. Amariah laughs.

Daniel's fist slams into Amariah's face yet again, sending more blood splattering on the steel tank behind him. A second punch sends even more blood, flying off the now bruised knuckles of Daniel, onto the console.

"I'll ask one last time," Daniel says. "Who the fuck hired you?" His fist cocking back for another punch. Amariah's hands slowly come up to cover his face.

"No more," he says through trembling hands. He takes several deep breaths, coughing several times and spitting out a glob of bloody spit. Daniel lets go of Amariah's thigh and stands up. He bends over and grabs Amariah loosely by the neck, lifting him to his feet. Daniel pins him to a tank with his forearm across Amariah's throat, making it tough for him to catch his breath.

Atany comes around the tank and gets in front of Amariah, looking him dead in the eyes. She stands there, silent, for a long while. She can see Amariah getting uncomfortable with her glare.

"Who hired you?" she asks with anger strong in her voice. She slaps him in the side of the head above Daniel's horizontal arm.

"Who the fuck hired you?" she screams at the top of her lungs, inches from his face, showering him in spittle as she screams.

Daniel tightens the pressure against Amariah's throat. He struggles to get air.

"The Rillian ambassador," Amariah says in between gasps of air. "The Rillian ambassador." His voice grows weaker. He body slumps under Daniel's arm.

Atany grabs each side of Amariah's jawbone with her hands, propping him against the tank as Daniel steps back a foot.

"Why did you do this, you piece of shit?" she screams at him. She gives him a hard knee to the gut. His body buckles under the force, and Atany forces him back upright, slamming his head against the metal tank he's propped against. She looks over and sees Abaddon.

"Drag this miserable fuck to the airlock," she tells two crewmen standing next to her.

They comply, each grabbing an arm. Amariah is too beaten to put up much of a fight. It takes less than a minute to get there. As he realizes what's about to happen, he starts to struggle. Atany walks up to him, staring him in the eyes.

"This is for Abaddon," she tells him as her knee violently slams into his genitals.

His eyes bulge as he strains to breathe, the intense pain shooting through his entire body. She gives him a little time for his brain to register the fullness of the pain. Her eyes lock onto his as they silently ask the last question she asked aloud.

"We were supposed to cripple the weapons systems," Amariah finally begins. "When we get home, the Rillian fleet is supposed to be waiting for us."

"Then why sabotage the vortex device?" she asks, gritting her teeth.

"Urania sabotaged the wrong components," he answers with contempt.

Atany nods to the crewman holding Amariah's left arm. He hits the control on the wall, and the airlock door opens. Amariah groggily turns his head when the door opens. His eyes grow wide. She nods again, and the two crewmen throw Amariah into the airlock, sealing the door behind him.

"Lieutenant Amariah," she says formally yet wearily, "you are guilty of sabotage, treason, and murder. I, Captain Dinema Atany, do sentence you to death." As she slaps the button on the wall, Amariah is blown out into the vacuum of space. Atany turns to face the group.

"Benjamin, get those fucking vortex components swapped," Atany commands as she stands tall, straightening her uniform. "Everyone get back to work. I'll be on the bridge. I want to be in Alliance space as soon as possible." She heads to the doorway, Daniel, Fental, and Torres behind her.

> *Captain's log, stardate 30125.61. The vortex device has been repaired, and we are ready to power it up and go home. We leave the Forzak homeworld for now, confident we will return. The battleship, named* Tartarus *by the crew, is holding together like it is brand-new, not a thousand years old.*

Atany sits on the bridge with Hawking in the seat beside her. The rest of the crew, both *Heaven*'s and *Deliverance*'s, are working together in unison.

"Engineering, full power to the vortex device," the captain orders. "Merah, open the vortex."

He complies, and the beam shoots out in front of the ship. Soon the spiraling vortex of darkness appears.

"Vortex fully opened, and power output is steady," Merah replies.

"Levi, bring us in."

"Yes, Captain," he says as he manipulates the controls. The ship starts to move toward to vortex.

"Penetrating the outer edge of the vortex," Fental announces.

"The ship is fully enveloped within the vortex," Fental announces after a few seconds. Several minutes later, the ship starts to be controlled by the computer.

"What do you think will be waiting for us on the other side?" Hawking asks Atany quietly.

"I don't know," she admits calmly. "But with this ship, it really doesn't matter." She sits back, a sly grin spreads across face.

About the Author

Born in 1963, R. N. Chevalier has been a fan of all sci-fi from an early age. Inspired by the moon landing unfolding before him, he became an instant fan, seeing fantasy become reality. This inspiration came to fruition with the release of his first novel, Are We the Klingons. This, second of a trilogy, is based on a board game invented by the author.

www.ingramcontent.com/pod-product-compliance
Lightning Source LLC
Chambersburg PA
CBHW071247210626
46818CB00013B/442